Jade Charlotte

Penalty Box

Copyright © 2025 by Jade Charlotte

All rights reserved. No part of this publication may be reproduced, stored or transmitted in any form or by any means, electronic, mechanical, photocopying, recording, scanning, or otherwise without written permission from the publisher. It is illegal to copy this book, post it to a website, or distribute it by any other means without permission.

This novel is entirely a work of fiction. The names, characters and incidents portrayed in it are the work of the author's imagination. Any resemblance to actual persons, living or dead, events or localities is entirely coincidental.

Jade Charlotte asserts the moral right to be identified as the author of this work.

First edition

This book was professionally typeset on Reedsy Find out more at reedsy.com

*For the ones who walked away—not to give up, but to grow.
For the hearts that chose healing, even when it meant letting someone go.
And for the love that stayed—flawed, quiet, unwavering.
Because sometimes you have to lose yourself to find your way back.
And sometimes, home isn't a place at all.
It's the person who never stopped waiting.
This is for you.*

Contents

Acknowledgments

Chapter 1

Chapter 2

Chapter 3

Chapter 4

Chapter 5

Chapter 6

Chapter 7

Chapter 8

Chapter 9

Chapter 10

Chapter 11

Chapter 12

Chapter 13

Chapter 14

Chapter 15

Chapter 16

Chapter 17

Chapter 18

Chapter 19

Chapter 20

Chapter 21

Chapter 22

Chapter 23

Chapter 24

Chapter 25

Chapter 26

Chapter 27

Chapter 28

Chapter 29

Chapter 30

Chapter 31

Chapter 32

Chapter 33

Chapter 34

Chapter 35

Chapter 36

Chapter 37

Chapter 38

Chapter 39

Chapter 40

Bonus Scene

Thank You for Reading

Acknowledgments

Writing this book stretched me in ways I didn't expect—and healed parts of me I didn't realize still needed it. So first, to the readers: thank you. For picking this book up. For giving it your time. For believing in slow burns, complicated emotions, and the kind of love that takes its time to grow.

If this story found you at the right moment, I hope it reminded you that it's okay to choose yourself. And that love—real love—won't fall apart when you do.

To my family: thank you for your constant support, your patience, and your belief in me when I struggled to believe in myself. Your love is what steadies me.

To my friends—you know who you are—thank you for cheering me on through every draft, every deleted scene, and every late-night panic message. You've listened, encouraged, and carried me through more than I can say. I'm endlessly grateful for you.

To my early readers, thank you for holding this book gently and helping me shape it into something stronger.

And finally, to anyone who's ever walked away to find themselves—this book is for you. Redemption isn't linear. Growth is rarely clean. But love that's rooted in honesty, in choice, in return? That's the kind worth writing for.

Thank you for letting me tell this story.

With love,
Jade

Chapter 1

Ethan

I should be happier than this.

That's what everyone keeps telling me. Or maybe it's what I keep telling myself.

It's a wedding. There's music, booze, people smiling like they mean it. The kind of night that's supposed to feel like a celebration.

But I'm not part of it.

I'm standing off to the side, bourbon in my hand, watching my dad kiss the woman who used to be mine.

And yeah, I'm happy for them.

At least, I want to be.

But it hurts more than I expected it to.

Lexi looks good. Peaceful in a way I never saw when we were together. Like she's not carrying anything heavy anymore. Her dress moves when the breeze picks up. Her smile holds steady, even when every part of me feels like it's starting to slip.

She was more than an ex. She was my best friend. The one who stayed longer than she should have, who tried harder than I deserved. The one who knew I was falling apart before I did.

And I still let her go.

Now she's here, dancing with my father in front of a hundred people, and everything about it feels right. Like they were always heading toward this and I was just in the way.

I take another sip of my drink. It doesn't help.

Their first dance starts. Some slow song I don't recognize. Everyone backs off to give them space. Phones go up. Smiles soften. Rachel's crying and pretending she's not.

Lexi's looking up at him with trust in her eyes.

And him?

He's looking at her like nothing else matters.

They kiss.

It's not dramatic. It's quiet. Simple.

Certain.

I should've left before this part. I thought about it.

But I didn't. And now I can't move.

Because all I can think is—

That should've been me.

Not with her. Not anymore.

But with someone.

Anyone.

Instead, I'm standing here with a drink I don't want, wearing a suit that doesn't fit right, trying to convince myself I'm not falling apart while everyone around me is building something.

And right now?

There's no one waiting for me.

Just an apartment that isn't mine and a reputation that follows me everywhere, no matter how much I try to outrun it.

I finish what's left in the glass. Too fast. Doesn't matter.

Somewhere nearby, Liam's yelling something about shots. Carter's trying too hard to charm the maid of honor. Connor's off to the side, looking at his phone like he's hoping someone texts back.

And me?

I'm watching my dad start the life I used to think I wanted—with the only person who ever really saw me.

And I've never felt more alone.

I don't remember leaving the wedding.

One second I was in the middle of sparklers, pretending to smile for the photographer while they kissed like no one else existed. The next, I was hunched over the bar in some place I didn't recognize, nursing a drink that burned but didn't numb anything.

I didn't mean to drink this much. That wasn't the plan.

Then again, I didn't really have one.

But watching Lexi walk down that aisle, hand in his, face soft and certain—

It cracked something open.

She used to look at me like that.

Before I fucked it all up. Before the late nights, the missed calls, the empty promises. Before I stopped being someone worth staying for.

I still don't know exactly when she stopped looking at me like I was worth it. I just remember the silence that followed.

And the guilt that never left.

Now I'm the guy at the bar, drinking too much and trying not to think about what it means that they're happier without me.

There's a group of girls nearby. They're laughing too loud. One of them says my name.

I hear it. I just don't care.

That used to be my thing. Let someone distract me for a few hours. Pretend the ache in my chest wasn't permanent. Hide the damage under someone else's lipstick and a clean exit.

But I can't stomach that tonight.

I'm tired. Of pretending I've got it together. Of being the guy people expect to mess it up. Lexi forgave me. My dad too. But it doesn't erase the fact that I burned bridges with both of them before I figured out how to stop setting fires.

They're both better off now.

I order another drink. It goes down easier than it should.

My phone buzzes in my pocket.

Connor.

I don't look at the screen. I already know what it says.

You good? Need a ride? Door's open.

We've been living together for the past few weeks. Since I sold the house, I haven't found the next place yet. Some guy came in with a full cash offer and wanted to close fast. No inspection. No strings. I took it.

I needed the clean break.

That place had started to feel like a monument to every bad choice I ever made. Too many late nights, too many empty mornings, too many bottles of bourbon I never should've opened in the first place.

Now my stuff's in storage, and I'm crashing at Connor's.

He offered. Said it was fine. Said he missed having someone else around.

He doesn't say it, but I think he's keeping an eye on me. Just in case.

Outside, the cold hits harder than expected. I didn't bring a jacket. Or maybe I forgot it somewhere.

I try to open the Uber app. The screen's too bright, and my fingers aren't cooperating.

I laugh once, under my breath. There's nothing funny about it.

I start walking.

Connor's building is only a few blocks away. I've walked this route plenty of times. It should feel familiar.

Tonight, it doesn't.

Everything feels distant. Like I'm watching myself from the outside. Like I've already disappeared, and nobody's noticed yet.

By the time I reach his door, I'm shivering.

The keypad blinks red when I punch in the code.

I squint, trying to focus. Try again.

Red again.

"Come on," I mutter. "Don't be like this."

I press the wrong number. Try to backspace. End up locking it out for thirty seconds.

I rest my forehead against the door and sigh.

Connor said he left it open. I'm sure he did. Or maybe I just wanted that to be true.

Either way, it's not opening.

I give up and slide down the door, legs out, head resting back against the wood.

Everything feels heavier in here. In my chest. In my arms. In my head.

I'm not proud of this moment.

I should text him. Ask him to let me in. But I don't trust myself to form words without spelling my own name wrong or saying something I'll regret in the morning.

I sit there, freezing.

And still, the ache doesn't go away.

The door unlocks.

I don't hear footsteps. Just the click. And then it opens behind me.

I fall backward into someone's legs.

Bare legs.

Not Connor's.

I look up.

She's standing in the doorway, one hand holding her phone, the other braced on the frame. Her eyes widen when she sees me.

She's not a stranger.

Not anymore.

"Avery?" My voice is rough. Slurred. "Is that... you?"

She frowns. "Are you trying to break into my brother's apartment?"

I try to sit up. Fail. My body's working against me. "He said it was open."

"Jesus. You're a mess."

"You're Connor's...?"

She crosses her arms. "Sister. It's been a few years, hasn't it?"

Right.

She was supposed to get in next week. Connor mentioned it once in passing.

Guess that timeline changed.

I groan and press the back of my hand to my forehead.

And then she bends down, grabs my arm, and starts hauling me inside.

She's stronger than she looks.

I don't fight her.

Chapter 2

Avery

Connor thought I was coming next week. That was the plan.

But plans stopped meaning anything the second everything I'd been holding together cracked wide open.

So I got on a plane.

No explanation. No warning. No long message that would make it worse.

I just needed out.

Away from my ex. Away from the PR fallout. Away from the goddamn whispers every time I walked into the training barn. I told my coach I needed time off, tossed a bag together, and booked the first flight that got me out of Florida.

And now I'm here.

Dragging my suitcase down the quiet hallway of Connor's building, completely exhausted and pretending I'm not about three minutes from either crying or throwing my phone into traffic.

The keypad beeps when I enter the code—his jersey number, my birthday, and the dumb goalie pun he thinks is clever. The lock clicks open.

Of course it does. He hasn't changed it in years.

The apartment is still. Clean. That kind of silence that feels curated, like everything in here exists just for show.

I step inside and close the door behind me. Drop my bag by the wall. Kick off my shoes and roll my neck until it cracks. I've been holding tension in my shoulders since last October, and it shows.

The bathroom light is soft. Warm. I don't bother turning on the overheads. Just strip out of my travel clothes and step into the shower before the decision can feel dramatic.

The water is scalding.

I let it burn anyway.

I've been in here less than ten minutes and I already feel like a stranger in my own skin.

The wine helps. So does the oversized t-shirt I changed into—worn and soft, with a sarcastic slogan that doesn't fit the mood.

But the silence isn't comfortable. It's heavy. Pressing in like it knows I didn't just come here to "clear my head."

I came here because I had nowhere else to go.

Because people looked at me like a liability instead of a rider.

Because a man I trusted turned me into a headline and smiled while he did it.

I pour a second glass of wine and lean against the counter, breathing through the sharp edge of the memory. My ex's voice still plays in my head sometimes. Cold. Practiced. Accusing me of being unstable. Difficult. Uncoachable.

And the worst part?

No one challenged him.

I take another sip and stare out the wide apartment windows. The city is loud in a way I forgot about—cars, horns, the occasional burst of laughter from the street below. But inside, it's all tension and glass.

I'm not staying here long. Just long enough to figure out what comes next. Maybe I'll take the new job offer. Maybe I'll quit riding altogether.

Right now, I just need quiet.

A chance to breathe without someone asking me for something.

The banging on the door starts just before midnight.

I freeze, glass halfway to my mouth.

Then I set it down and cross the room slowly, bare feet silent on the floor.

Another thump. Then swearing. A low voice. The keypad beeps twice and blinks red through the peephole.

I grab my phone and call the only person who should be anywhere near this apartment right now.

Connor answers on the second ring. "Avery are you okay?"

"Hey." I pause. "Surprise. I came home early."

He's quiet for a beat. "Oh okay, are you good?"

"Yes but someone is currently trying to break into your apartment."

Another pause. "Shit. It's Ethan, hes not had a good day and hes staying with me while he looks for another place, his last house just sold."

I blink. "Oh right."

"Yeah."

"Well what do you want me to do?"

"Can you let him in? Make sure he doesn't drown himself in alcohol until I get back?"

"I don't know, should I? Or should I call building security and let them deal with your emotionally unavailable friend?"

"Please, Aves."

I sigh. "Fine. But you owe me."

"Deal."

I hang up and open the door.

Ethan Wilson promptly falls backward into my legs.

And he's a mess.

One boot half off, suit wrinkled, hair a disaster. He blinks up at me like I'm a hallucination he isn't ready to process.

I look down at him, unimpressed.

"Avery? Is that... you?"

"Are you trying to break into my brother's apartment?"

"He said it was open."

"Jesus. You're a mess."

"You're Connor's...?"

"Sister. It's been a few years, hasn't it?"

He groans and drops his head back against the frame like he might pass out right there.

I should've left him on the floor.

But instead, I reach down and catch his elbow before he tips sideways.

"Yeah," I mutter, half to myself. "This week's going great."

He sways. I pull.

And together, we stumble back inside—me, barefoot and annoyed. Him, drunk and heavier than he looks.

Connor owes me.

Big time.

Chapter 3

Avery

Dragging six feet of drunken hockey player through my brother's apartment was not on my bingo card for the week.

Ethan groans as I yank him toward the bathroom, his full weight dragging against me like he's trying to make this harder on purpose.

"You're very heavy," I mutter.

"You're very small," he slurs, head tilting toward me like that's supposed to be charming.

"Wow," I say. "A compliment and an insult. Off to a great start."

He lets out a low laugh, then nearly takes out the hallway mirror. I grab his arm before he faceplants. My fingers wrap around his bicep and I try not to register how solid it is. Try being the key word.

"What the hell are you bench pressing—team trauma?"

He doesn't answer, but his mouth twitches.

I shove open the bathroom door with my shoulder. Connor's spa nightmare of a bathroom—glass, stone, and enough ambient light to expose all your emotional flaws.

I flick the water on and steer Ethan toward the shower.

He drops to his knees with a groan.

"You're welcome," I mutter, and push him fully under the stream.

Cold water hits him first. He jolts and swears, flinching like I've slapped him.

"Jesus!" he sputters. "You trying to kill me?"

"Tempting. But no. This is just how we do interventions in this family."

He looks miserable. Hair soaked, shirt plastered to his chest, eyes struggling to focus. He tries to undo the buttons, but his hands are useless.

"Move over, disaster," I sigh. "I'll help."

"You gonna undress me?" he grins. "Is this... strip shower care?"

"Don't make it weird."

But it already is.

I unfasten his shirt quickly, hands steady even though my brain is not. Once I peel the wet fabric away, I drop it onto the tile with a heavy slap. His chest rises and falls slowly like every breath is work.

"Pants?"

He nods, barely.

I get them off fast and clinical. He's in boxers—gray, fitted, and yes, I notice. I pretend I don't.

I sit back on the edge of the tub, reach for my wine glass, and try not to look at him again.

"You're really quiet all of a sudden," he says without opening his eyes.

"I'm restraining myself from kicking you for getting this drunk."

"I appreciate your restraint."

He tilts his head under the spray, letting it run over his face.

"You're good at this."

"At what?"

"Taking care of people who don't deserve it."

"I'm not taking care of you," I say. "This is controlled tolerance."

"Hmmm, you've changed," he murmurs.

I glance at him. "So have you."

"You were quieter back then."

"I was young."

His voice drops. "You're beautiful."

My chest pulls tight.

I should brush it off. Make a joke. But I don't.

Because he says it like it's not a line. Like he's only just now letting himself admit it out loud.

"I know what people think of me," he adds. "That I'm the guy who messes everything up. That I don't care enough. That I'm not serious about my career, about anything."

His voice is softer now.

"They still see the version of me from two years ago. Doesn't matter what I do now. It's like they're just waiting for me to screw it up again."

I stare at the tile.

Then I say, "He told them I was unstable."

Ethan looks at me.

"My ex," I add. "Said I was too emotional. Impossible to coach. He made sure people heard that first—and believed it."

I take another sip of wine, slower this time.

"I lost almost everything. Sponsors, placements, trust. I didn't even fight it. I was just... tired. Of defending myself. Of pretending I was fine."

I shift my legs up onto the tub, curling in on myself a little.

"I'm so sick of hurting. So sick of being something people talk about instead of talk to."

He's quiet for a long time.

Then, gently—"Yeah. I get that."

We're not strangers. Not really. We've known of each other for years. Exchanged polite conversations in hallways. Sat at the same table a handful of times. He was always just one orbit out of reach. And now... he's right here.

I move to stand and nearly slip.

His hand snaps out fast, catching my waist. His grip is steady, solid, and before I can blink, I'm off-balance and in his lap—knees bracketing his hips, hand planted on his chest, the other catching the edge of the tile wall.

We freeze.

Water pours down over both of us.

He holds me like he's afraid I'll pull away.

But I don't.

"I should go," I whisper.

"Don't."

His hand rests on my thigh. Warm, grounded. No pressure. But he's not letting go either. His other hand slides to my waist. Gentle. Like I'm something he's scared to break.

"This is a bad idea," I murmur, even as I shift slightly, adjusting in his lap.

"The worst," he says.

"You can tell me to stop," he adds, voice steady. "And I will."

I don't say it.

Instead, I stay.

And I lean in.

When our mouths meet, it's slow. Intentional. There's no game in it—just something honest, something full of everything we've both been keeping locked behind polite smiles and tired eyes.

His lips are soft, but the kiss deepens fast. Urgent. Heated.

My body moves closer before I even register it. His arm wraps around my back, pulling me into him. My hands find his shoulders. I kiss him like I mean it.

Like I need it.

His hand slips under my shirt, dragging over damp skin, across my ribs. My hips press tighter into his. His breath hitches when I rock against him.

"We don't really know each other," I say, forehead pressed to his.

"We know enough," he says.

And he's right. Maybe we haven't had long talks or shared secrets before tonight, but somehow, we've both always understood each other.

His hand curves around the back of my thigh, pulling me tighter.

Then he breathes into my neck—wrecked and real.

"I just need to feel something real that isn't falling apart."

The words hit something deep in me.

I press my mouth to his again. Not just hunger now—connection.

His other hand slips under the waistband of my underwear.

I gasp as his fingers stroke over me—slow and reverent.

He doesn't rush.

Just touches me like I'm something worth learning.

"Ethan—" My voice breaks.

"You're incredible," he breathes. "So warm. So soft."

His mouth moves to my throat, kissing gently as his fingers slide through the slick heat between my legs.

I rock into him, barely conscious of anything beyond the way he holds me.

His mouth moves to my throat, kissing gently as his fingers slide through the slick heat between my legs. I shudder at the contact, everything inside me pulling tighter.

He doesn't rush. Doesn't push. Just keeps touching me like he's trying to learn what I like by feel alone.

My hips shift, grinding into his palm. His breath catches, and his hand slides further under my shirt, fingers tracing the curve of my waist, moving slowly, deliberately.

"You're so fucking soft," he whispers, voice low and uneven. "I can't stop touching you."

I arch into him as his mouth trails lower—down my throat, along my collarbone—hot breath against soaked cotton. Then lower.

His lips close around the peak of my breast through the wet fabric, and I gasp, grabbing at his shoulders, grounding myself with my fingers digging into his skin.

He sucks lightly, tongue dragging across the fabric just enough to make my back arch and my thighs tense around his hips. His hand keeps stroking between my legs—slow, steady pressure that's winding me tighter with every breath.

The fabric of my shirt clings to me, water making everything translucent and clumsy, but he doesn't care. Neither do I.

He sucks again, this time harder, and my head tips back with a strangled moan. My body is so wound up I can barely think. He's everywhere—his hands, his mouth, his voice breaking in my ear like he's falling apart right along with me.

"You're driving me insane," he says, fingers pressing deeper.

I feel like I'm burning.

And I don't want it to stop.

His tongue circles my nipple through the cotton, teasing until my breath comes fast and shallow, and I'm not sure I've ever needed anything as badly as I need him to keep going. My hand slides into his hair, wet strands curling between my fingers, as I hold him to me, not ready to let go.

"Your what I didn't know I needed," he murmurs against my chest, voice so low I almost don't catch it.

He presses a kiss just beneath the hem of my shirt, then slides his fingers back up between my thighs—two of them now, stroking deeper. My body jerks with it, tension curling and coiling inside me until I can't hold it anymore.

"Ethan—" My voice breaks again, higher this time. "I'm—"

"I know," he breathes. "Let go. I've got you."

And I do.

I come in his lap with a moan that tears out of me, my body shaking as the pleasure takes over. I bury my face in his neck, clinging to him, unable to think or move or breathe until the wave passes.

He keeps holding me—arms around my waist, mouth brushing my hair, chest rising fast under my hands.

Neither of us speaks.

The silence isn't awkward. It's thick. Safe.

And for the first time in weeks, maybe months, I don't feel like I'm falling apart.

I feel... held.

By someone who actually knows how.

His arms stay around me.

We don't move. Not right away.

My head rests on his shoulder, breath still uneven, heart pounding against his chest. He doesn't rush me. Doesn't say anything. Just keeps his hands where they are—steady, sure, holding me like I'm something worth staying for.

Eventually, I lift my head.

His eyes are already on me.

Not smug. Not hungry. Just... present.

There's water still dripping from his hair, sliding down his jaw. His lips are parted, but he doesn't speak. Not yet.

My palm finds his cheek. I don't think about it. I just touch him.

He leans into it, like that's the thing that breaks him.

"I've always known you saw me different," he says quietly.

I blink. "What do you mean?"

"You never gave a shit about the rest of it. The money. The name. Who my dad is. You didn't care if I was first line or scratched from the roster. You've always just... seen me."

My throat tightens.

"I think I hated you for that at first," he adds, a breath of a laugh slipping out. "Because you didn't fall for the show."

I smile, small and tired. "You've always been insufferable."

He nods, grinning slightly. "Yeah. And you've always made it really clear you weren't impressed."

"Still not."

"That's why I trust you."

The words land harder than I expect.

We stare at each other. Close. Too close.

But there's no discomfort in it now.

Only this strange, quiet clarity.

He cups my jaw with one hand, thumb brushing my cheek. His voice drops even lower.

"This feels right," he says.

And God, it does.

I lean in.

He meets me there.

The kiss is slow this time. Less heat. More meaning. His mouth moves over mine like we've done this a thousand times and somehow it still matters. It's not about distraction anymore.

It's about choosing this.

Choosing each other.

His hand stays at my cheek. Mine slides to the back of his neck. I open to him, let him in, and for once, I don't overthink what happens next.

Because I don't need to.

For the first time in months, this doesn't feel like a mistake.

It feels like breathing.

Then—

The front door opens.

We freeze.

Footsteps. Connor's voice, casual and close.

"Ethan? Avery?"

I scramble off his lap, heart pounding, skin still flushed and wet. I grab the nearest towel and wrap it around myself like it might protect me from whatever happens next.

Ethan leans back against the tile, jaw set, eyes unreadable.

Connor appears in the doorway.

He stops cold.

His gaze flicks between the water on the floor, Ethan in boxers, and me—dripping wet, towel-wrapped, face burning.

His brows draw together. "Why are you wet?"

I stare at him, deadpan. "Because I had to help him into the shower."

Connor blinks once. "Right. Why did he need a shower?"

I cross my arms, towel tightening. "He could barely walk."

"She dragged me," Ethan adds, voice casual. Too casual. "Didn't give me a choice."

Connor raises an eyebrow. "You look conscious enough now."

"She sobered me up. Little firecracker usually does."

My head snaps toward him.

He's got the nerve to give me that lazy smirk—like nothing just happened. Like he wasn't whispering how good I felt two minutes ago.

Connor, of course, doesn't blink.

He just shakes his head. "You two still hate each other, huh?"

"Some things are eternal," Ethan says lightly.

"I'll never understand your friendship," Connor mutters.

"It's not a friendship, its just tolerance for your team mates," I snap before I can stop myself.

Ethan's expression doesn't change, but I feel the shift. His wall goes back up completely.

Connor yawns, glancing at his watch. "Alright. I'm heading to bed. Avery, thanks for saving this idiot from himself."

I nod stiffly.

Connor pauses, then gestures at the floor. "Try not to flood the place."

He walks off, completely unfazed, and disappears down the hall.

Silence stretches.

I turn to Ethan, the words rising in my throat—sharp, confused, maybe angry.

But before I can say anything, he speaks first.

"I'm sorry."

His voice stops me cold.

"I shouldn't have touched you. I got caught up. You were right there and I just... I wasn't thinking."

I stare at the floor. Water drips from my hair onto the tile. My fingers tighten around the edge of the towel.

"I can't do that. Not with you. Not when you're—"

He pauses. "Connor's sister."

That's it.

That's all I get.

Not a single word about what it meant. Not even a flicker of acknowledgment that maybe—just maybe—it meant something at all.

I nod once. Small. Almost imperceptible.

Then I turn.

And I walk out of the bathroom.

No parting shot. No sarcasm.

Just silence.

The kind that sinks in and settles deep.

I make it to the guest room, close the door gently behind me, and lean against it for a second—like that might hold me up.

It doesn't.

I slide the towel from my body and drop it to the floor. Grab a t-shirt from my bag and pull it over my head with shaking hands. My skin still smells like him. Like steam and sweat and something I let myself believe was real for half a second.

Stupid.

I climb into bed and pull the covers up around me, curling in on myself.

Not because I'm cold.

Because for a moment tonight, I thought he saw me.

And now I know better.

Chapter 4

Ethan

The first thing I feel is my spine screaming.

The second is the taste of stale regret in my mouth.

I groan and shift on the couch, which turns out to be a mistake. My neck's twisted, my shoulder's numb, and I'm pretty sure my body has been shaped around a throw pillow. There's a towel half-draped over my legs. Leather couch. Too short. I blink at the ceiling and try to remember how I got here.

Connor's apartment.

Right.

The headache hits me second, then the full body ache. Then the memory.

The shower. Her legs. Her voice.

Avery.

I sit up too fast, wince, and scrub a hand over my face. There's an empty glass of water and two aspirin sitting on the coffee table like someone tried to help me out. I don't remember taking them. I don't remember getting out of the shower.

But I remember everything else.

Avery in my lap. Her hand in my hair. Her mouth. Her body under mine.

And then Connor's voice. The towel. Her shouting. Storming off without looking back.

I drag the towel higher on my lap, not that it matters now. Nothing about last night can be undone.

I shouldn't have touched her. I was drunk. Exhausted. Too raw to make good choices. And she's Connor's sister.

I press the heel of my hand to my eye socket like pressure can erase memory.

From down the hall, I hear a door shut. Cabinets open in the kitchen, a little louder than necessary. She's awake.

I stay where I am for another minute, shirt wrinkled on the floor beside me. Still damp. I pick it up and pull it on. Leave it unbuttoned. No point pretending this morning is clean when last night already happened.

My phone buzzes. One new message.

Dad:

Hope you got home safe. Thank you for everything. Yesterday was the best day of our lives. We're proud of you.

I read it twice.

Proud.

I want to feel good about that. I want to hold on to it.

But all I can think about is the part that came after.

I put the phone down and walk into the kitchen.

She's there. Hoodie. Mug in hand. Eyes on the far wall.

"Morning," I say. My voice sounds worse than I expected.

She doesn't look at me. "Hi."

I lean against the counter. The silence isn't friendly. It's sharp around the edges.

"Look," I start, "about last night—"

"Which part?" she asks, setting the mug down. "The part where you pulled me into the shower with you are the part where you pretty much told me I was one of your stupid mistakes?"

My stomach turns. "I didn't know what else to say."

"Of course you didn't."

She still doesn't look at me.

"I was drunk, Avery. It wasn't planned. It wasn't even— You are his sister... his little sister. What sort of friend would I be if I pursued you?"

"You already did something though!" she says, cutting me off. "But its okay on your terms?"

I don't answer that. Not directly.

"You're Connor's sister," I say.

"Yeah, you keep saying that. Like it excuses you wanting to pretend none of it happened. I bared my soul to you, told you how my ex treated me, and they you go and do that."

She crosses her arms. Her face is flushed, but her voice stays steady.

"I don't normally do stuff like that," she says. "I don't hook up with guys who are emotionally wrecked and half-dressed in my brother's bathroom."

"Neither do I," I mutter.

"You are full of shit" she fires back.

I don't rise to it.

She lets out a breath and turns away again. Grabs the coffee pot, even though her mug is already full.

I try to keep it steady. "I'm not proud of what happened. But I'm not exactly sorry either."

She finally looks at me.

And it's not anger in her eyes. Not completely.

It's disappointment.

"You don't get to say that," she tells me. "Not after acting like it meant nothing. Not after acting like I was just another bad decision."

"I didn't mean it like that."

"No?" she asks. "Because you acted like I was just... convenient. Like it didn't cost you anything to touch me and then pretend you hadn't."

I open my mouth to answer, but she turns her back before I can say a word.

"Your shirt's on inside out," she adds.

I look down. She's right.

Before I can fix it, Connor walks into the room.

"Morning," he says, completely unfazed. "How's everyone?"

Avery doesn't answer. She moves to the fridge like she's looking for something to throw.

"Good," I say quickly.

Connor grabs the orange juice and pours himself a glass. "You look like shit, by the way."

"Thanks."

He takes a sip and glances between us. "So. Last night was... something."

Avery closes the fridge a little too hard.

I try to laugh it off. "Nothing like getting locked out, huh?"

Connor chuckles. "Yeah, thanks for helping him," he says to her. "Seriously."

She shrugs, eyes locked on the countertop.

"I was out cold," I say, trying to match the energy. "She saved my life."

"She's good like that," Connor replies. "She usually dislikes you, though. Maybe you caught her on a good day. I kinda wish you two got on better, all these years and you've never really seen eye to eye. Maybe you should get to know each other better, you know my favorite sister and my best friend, be nice to not worry you are going to throttle each other."

Avery's head turns. "I am your only sister, so that's not really a compliment. And maybe I don't like him because hes self absorbed and thinks hes gods gift. Which you're not, by the way." She looks directly at me.

"Anyway," he says, setting his glass in the sink trying to avoid any confrontation. "We've got practice. Let's go, Ethan."

He grabs his gear bag from the hallway, already in motion.

"Catch you later, sis."

I glance at her one last time.

She doesn't look at me. Doesn't move.

Just stands there, one hand braced on the counter, the other holding her mug so tight I'm surprised it doesn't crack.

I follow Connor out the door.

The hallway's quiet. My footsteps feel too loud.

And all I can think about is the look she gave me.

Like I was exactly the version of myself she hoped I wouldn't be.

Chapter 5

Avery

I make it all the way down the hall before I let myself react.

One more second of pretending I'm fine.

One more second of smiling politely while my brother—my *actual* biological brother—says things like *"I wish you two would get along"* as if I haven't *already* been on top of his best friend in a high-pressure aquatic situation.

My hand trembles on the doorknob. I close the guest room door behind me, lean back against it, and take a breath.

Then I let it out in the form of a very quiet, very violent pillow scream.

Because I *can't*.

I cannot.

He smirked. Ethan freaking Wilson smirked at me in the kitchen like we didn't almost invent a new category of poor judgment the night before. Like my legs hadn't been wrapped around his hips and my hand in his hair while water poured down around us while he ha his fingers inside me.

And Connor turns to us and is like... *"You should get to know each other."*

Sure, Connor. Want to know what your best friend's mouth tastes like? Because I do.

Oh my God.

I press both hands to my face and drag them down like it'll squeeze the memory out through my pores.

Then I rip off my hoodie, yank on something clean— leggings, a fresh hoodie and fluffy socks—and grab my phone like it's my last remaining lifeline.

Mia.

She picks up on the first ring.

"Whats up babes?" she says.

"I just shared a shower with my brother's best friend."

Pause.

"...I'm sorry. You what?"

I groan and flop onto my back, staring at the ceiling.

"Connor's best friend. Ethan Wilson. Hockey player. Six feet of tragic energy and emotional baggage in boxers."

"Hold on—Ethan? The guy who punches people for fun and used to be in every second tabloid headline last season?"

"*That* Ethan."

"Oh my *God.* Tell me everything. OH MY GOD! I thought you didn't like him?"

"I helped him into the shower to sober up and then— things may have happened. And I thought I didn't like him too."

"Avery, this is so funny! Did you and him have shower intercourse?"

"I didn't sleep with him!"

"But something happened?"

"Technically."

"OH YES"

"There was touching. But he was drunk and I was sad, and maybe had a few too many glasses of wine."

"Avery." All I hear is Mia laughing down the phone.

I groan. "He pulled me in! I was trying to leave and he yanked me into his lap like a badly timed rom-com."

"I love this!"

I bury my face in the pillow.

"This morning," I mumble, "he had the *audacity* to walk into the kitchen and act like *nothing happened.* Like he didn't try to steam-seduce me while I was doing humanitarian work. And continued telling me it can't happen anyway, because of Connor."

Mia gasps. "Oh babes."

"I know."

"And Connor?"

"He thinks we should be friends because we are two important people in his life."

Mia wheezes. "Does he know you let his best friend put his fingers inside your…"

"I'm hanging up."

"No, you're not. You *owe* me this drama."

I roll over, exasperated and still damp. "I've sworn off athletes."

"Uh-huh."

"Especially hot ones with anger issues."

"You mean the ones who seduce you in showers?"

"It's literally happened *once!*"

"We will see."

I groan. "I hate you."

"You love me. Now tell me: on a scale from 1 to 'you're definitely going to make out again,' where are we at?"

"Remind me why we're friends?"

"Because I support your journey. Now go hydrate. You've got a long day of passive-aggressively avoiding sexual tension ahead of you."

I hang up.
And then I lie there in silence.

Chapter 6

Ethan

Connor's standing in front of the fridge, eating cheese straight from the block.

"How's your head?" he asks, not turning around.

"Still recovering." I lean against the counter, squinting at the fluorescent light. "Was I an absolute disaster?"

He shrugs. "I've seen worse. You didn't puke. No property damage."

"Low bar."

He grins. "Your pride took the biggest hit."

"Temporary injury. Should bounce back."

"Classic Wilson."

He finally shuts the fridge and tosses me a Gatorade. I catch it and twist the cap, sipping slowly. My body still feels like hell from practice, and my head's not much better. Between the drinking, the ice time, and everything I'm not saying out loud, I'm barely holding it together.

Connor grabs a protein bar and leans against the opposite counter.

"You skated hard today," he says. "Didn't expect that after the way you looked this morning."

"I needed the sweat."

He nods. "Coach noticed. Said you looked sharp."

"I'm locked in this year," I tell him. "No distractions. I'm not screwing around."

"That's good," he says. "It's a big year. For all of us."

There's a pause. Just long enough to feel intentional.

He unwraps the protein bar, doesn't eat it right away.

"I know you and Avery haven't always gotten along," he says casually. "You've never been close. I get it—your personalities don't exactly click."

I don't respond.

He continues, easy but clear. "She's staying here for a bit. Just wanted to ask you to keep things easy while she's around."

"I wasn't planning to make it hard," I say.

"I know. You never have. I trust you."

He means it.

"And I know nothing's going on," he adds quickly. "I'm not implying that. I just figured it's worth saying once—before we all get too comfortable with hallway run-ins and shared laundry space. Shes off limits."

"I get it."

"She's had a rough year," he says. "With her ex, with her career. She doesn't need more complications."

"I'm not trying to be one."

"I know, and it would be nice if you two finally got along. You both mean a lot to me."

"You mean a lot to me too pal."

He heads toward the hallway, pulling on a hoodie. "Video review's in twenty. You still skipping?"

"Yeah. Headache."

"Drink more water."

He grabs his keys, opens the door, then stops and glances back once more.

"And don't shoot glove side next practice. You're not getting past me there."

I let out a tired breath. "You sure about that?"

He grins. "You score on me again, I'm blaming Avery for throwing you off your game."

He leaves without waiting for a response.

And I just stand there in the kitchen, staring at the spot he was just in.

He doesn't know.

He doesn't suspect anything.

He trusts me.

And all I can think about is how close I came to shattering that trust completely.

Chapter 7

Ethan

It's been three days since we last spoke.

We've shared the same kitchen, the same hallway, passed each other in silence more than once—but neither of us has acknowledged what happened. There's been no yelling. No apology. Just space. Cold and stretched thin between us like a drawn line we both know not to cross.

I've been living here a few weeks now. Avery's only been here a few days, but somehow it already feels like she owns more of this place than I do. And I can't stop thinking about the look on her face after the shower. Not the part where she kissed me back. Not the part where she moaned my name.

The part where she walked away like she couldn't believe she let it happen.

Now it's 7:30AM, and I'm making pancakes.

It's stupid, I know that. But it's something. Something that isn't silence. Something that says I don't want this to stay broken.

I heard her door open twenty minutes ago.

I flip a pancake and try to keep my breathing even.

She walks in a minute later. Hoodie. Sweatpants. Hair up. Tired eyes. No makeup.

She stops when she sees me. Doesn't move.

"Morning," I say.

Her expression doesn't change. "What are you doing?"

"Making pancakes."

She eyes the stove. Then the plate. Then back at me.

"Why?"

"Because I figured we both live here. And eating pancakes in silence is better than pretending we don't exist."

She walks in slowly. Picks up a fork from the counter. Cuts into the top pancake, chews, swallows.

"They're fine."

"I'll take it."

She eats another bite. Then sets the fork down and leans back on the counter.

"You don't have to make me breakfast just because I ended up in your lap and you regret it now."

I shake my head. "That's not what this is."

"Then what is it?"

"I don't know," I admit. "A truce, maybe. Some kind of normal."

She watches me. "You grabbed me."

"I was trying to stop you from falling. You slipped."

"And I happen to land in your lap."

"Okay maybe I pulled you in a little. And I should've let go."

"But you didn't."

"No," I say. "I didn't."

The silence stretches. Not heavy. Just real.

She takes another sip of coffee. Doesn't look at me.

"I shouldn't have kissed you."

"I kissed you back."

She doesn't argue. Just folds her arms over her chest and looks down at the counter.

"I don't do messy," she says. "Not anymore. I don't want to be someone's mistake."

"You're not."

"Feels like it. You touched me, kissed me and made me feel something and then changed as soon as Connor walked in."

I exhale slowly. "Look, Connor trusts me. I've known him longer than anyone on that team. He's been there through everything. Every time I crashed, he didn't walk away."

She finally looks at me.

"And I'd never do anything to break that."

Her jaw tightens. "Then don't."

"I'm trying, but I don't think what happened was a mistake. It felt different with you. It felt easy, it felt good. In another life maybe we could have..."

"Don't."

"Please let me try to make this right."

She finishes her coffee and sets the mug down.

"I don't hate you," she says. "But I don't trust you. And I don't want more chaos in my life. So I will be civil for Connor, but that's it."

"I'm not trying to be chaos."

She gives me a look. "You're Ethan Wilson."

I nod once. "Yeah. I am."

She picks up the fork again, eats another bite.

"They need more syrup," she says quietly.

She turns and walks out of the kitchen.

I glance over my shoulder.

"You know," I say, "you really ruin a good guilt spiral when you talk like that."

She smiles. A tiny, evil smile. "I'm not here to make your spirals easier."

God help me, I grin back.

Chapter 8

Avery

Living in your older brother's apartment is already a low-grade nightmare. Living in your older brother's apartment while his emotionally complicated best friend lives in the spare room two doors down? That's the kind of psychological test they build military simulations around.

It's been three days since Ethan tried to apologise in the form of pancakes that somehow both sucked and meant something. We haven't really spoken since. Just awkward near-collisions in the hallway and shared silences over breakfast while Connor obliviously monologues about protein ratios and team drama.

This morning, I'm in the kitchen reheating coffee when Connor walks in holding two bananas and a clear sense of purpose.

"Family meeting," he says, tossing one banana onto the counter like it's a grenade.

I eye him. "He's not our family."

Connor grins. "And yet here we all are. Living together. Under one very expensive roof that I pay for, by the way."

"Wow. Subtle flex."

He gestures for me to sit at the island. I do, mostly because I'm curious what flavor of chaos he's selling today.

Ethan strolls in a second later, sleep-rumpled and still radiating faint cologne and hockey-player exhaustion. His shirt clings in all the wrong places. Or the right ones. I haven't decided yet.

He blinks at us. "What's happening?"

"Family meeting," Connor says again.

Ethan sighs and drops into the chair next to mine. I try not to lean away. I also try not to *lean toward him*. I succeed at neither.

Connor claps once. "Okay. Ground rules. This house is a sacred space of healing and recovery. I am the Switzerland of emotional disasters. You are both in a very delicate state of psychological rebirth—"

"Did you eat one of your pre-workout scoops *dry* again?" I interrupt.

"Let him finish," Ethan mutters, rubbing his eyes. "This is the most structure I've had all week."

Connor beams. "Thank you. Now. Rule number one: don't be awkward with each other."

"Define awkward," I say, because I know damn well what he's trying to prevent.

Connor gestures between us. "I'm saying no passive aggression. No dramatic sighing in the hallway. Just stop hating on each other., you don't even know each other."

"I don't hate him," I say.

"Yeah," Ethan adds, "Because it feels like you really like me right now."

Connor gives us the world's flattest look. "You two are like emotionally constipated magnets. I swear, I walk into a room and I *feel* the tension between you."

"I'm not tense," I lie.

Ethan shrugs. "I'm kind of always tense."

"Right," Connor says. "Which brings me to rule number two: you don't have to be friends. But I would love it if you could at least *pretend* not to hate each other. Maybe talk sometimes. Like humans. You are both healing in your own way, and neither of you have done anything wrong to the other person."

"Define talk," Ethan says, voice low, with a sideways glance that brushes heat across my collarbone.

Connor groans. "Jesus Christ, you're impossible."

"I'm trying," Ethan says, looking directly at me now. "I made her pancakes."

"She said they were burnt," Connor replies.

"She ate two."

"I *was hungry*," I snap.

"Exactly," Ethan says, all smug and *barefoot*, which feels somehow worse than being shirtless. "I filled a need."

Connor holds up both hands. "Okay, great, so we're all devolving. Awesome." Then he heads to the 'hockey room' as I like to call it and grabs his stuff for practice.

Ethan's still watching me when Connor reappears, gear bag in one hand, helmet in the other.

"Wilson," he calls, tossing a granola bar over the counter. "Let's go. We're gonna be late."

"Yep, thanks Mom." Ethan says, standing up and grabbing his bag.

Connor ignores him and looks at me. "You need anything while we're out? Food? Sanity?"

"I'm good."

"You sure?"

I nod. He nods back, but there's a flicker of concern under his usual chaos.

"Call me if you need to," he says. "I'll text when we're heading home later, it might be a late one because the season is about to start and we have a lot to go over."

"Yeah okay. Have fun."

He heads for the door. Ethan lingers a beat behind him, looking at me like he wants to say something but can't figure out which version of himself is allowed to talk to me now.

"Try not to break anything," He smirks at me.

"No promises." I manage to reply.

And then they're gone.

Silence settles like dust in the apartment.

I stare at the counter.

And then my phone rings.

Blocked number.

I stare at it for a second.

Then I answer.

"...Hello?"

"Avery. It's Dan."

His voice drops me right back into the arena—dirt under my boots, clipboard in his hand, a stopwatch and a lecture about pacing. Coach Dan Mallory. My old trainer. One of the few people who didn't immediately jump ship when the tabloids got messy.

"I've got something for you," he says. "Something real good."

I sit down. "Go on."

"There's a position opening in Louisiana. A competitive stable. Full-time. Paid. They've got national-level clients and one of their head trainers is stepping down in three months. They want someone to start overlapping soon—

training under her, transitioning in smoothly. You will have opportunities to compete over there."

My heart jumps and drops at the same time.

"Is this a real offer?" I ask.

"It's real. They've seen your tapes. They know the situation. They don't care about the headlines."

I close my eyes. "And when would they want me to start?"

"I need to give them a yes or no by the end of next week," he says. "But the job wouldn't officially start until summer. Gives you three months to prep, move, finish whatever you're doing now."

Three months.

Three months in this apartment.

Three months of early mornings, weird silences, and Ethan Wilson being... here.

Dan keeps talking. "It's not the Olympic pipeline, I'll be honest. But it's a way back in. A clean one."

"I get it," I say. "I just—I need time to think."

"You've got it. But not much. One week."

He hangs up, and I stare at the wall for a long time.

Three months.

Chapter 9

Avery

It's just a night out. Some drinks, some banter, a table full of hockey players trying too hard and puck bunnies worming their way in.

But I'm still here in front of the mirror in Connor's annoyingly perfect guest bathroom, adjusting the hem of a black dress that fits like I planned this. Like I care. Like I know what I'm doing.

It's not scandalous. Not even flashy. Just clean lines, smooth fabric, and a cut that says I picked this on purpose.

I didn't. But I need to feel like I did.

The heels go on next—tall and sharp, not made for comfort. The kind you wear when you want to be seen. My hair's loose around my shoulders, soft waves falling with the kind of effort that's supposed to look effortless. A little liner, mascara, and a spritz of something expensive.

I don't look like the girl who spent days avoiding eye contact in her own hallway.

I don't look like the girl who keeps remembering the sound Ethan made when I rocked against his lap in a shower built for better decisions.

I look fine.

More than fine.

There's a knock at the door. "You ready?" Connor calls.

I take one last look at myself.

"I'm ready." Thankfully Ethan was meeting us there because he went straight from practice. But Connor came home to pick me up.

The bar is loud the second we walk in—dim lights, thick bass, and the kind of energy that makes you forget it's only a Wednesday. The team has already claimed a long booth in the back.

I've known most of them for years. Not well. Not like this. Just enough to recognize names, voices, the way they move on the ice. I've been in the stands. At dinners. I've heard the stories. But I've never really been *part* of it. Not until tonight.

I spot Liam immediately, halfway through what looks like a dramatic re-enactment of something involving nachos. Carter is leaning into a waitress' personal space, all charm and no self-awareness. And Ethan's at the edge of the booth, one arm slung across the backrest, beer in hand, half-smile in place like nothing ever phases him.

He sees me.

And for a second, he just... stares.

Not surprised. Not smug. Just quiet. Focused. Like he didn't expect me to actually show up, but now that I'm here, he doesn't know where to look first.

I hold his gaze for a beat too long. He looks away first. Takes a drink. Shifts like maybe sitting still suddenly feels harder than it should.

Connor touches my arm, light. "Thanks for coming."

"Bit of fun, right?"

"Exactly."

We walk toward the table together. I feel the heat of Ethan's eyes again before we even reach the end of the booth.

That's when the women notice me.

Three of them. All confidence and laughter and perfect makeup that somehow hasn't moved all night. The one who stands first is petite, brunette, and smiling like we already know each other.

"Avery?" she says.

I nod. "That's me."

She hugs me without hesitation. "Finally. I've been dying to meet Connor's little sister."

I blink. "That's the legacy I'm leaving?"

"Could be worse," she says. "I'm Lexi."

And that's when it clicks. She's the one. Ethan's ex. The one from the wedding.

Of course she's beautiful.

She steps back, and the other two wave.

"This is Maya," Lexi says, motioning to the one with slicked-back hair and sniper eyes. "And Rachel."

Rachel lifts her drink in greeting, nails painted the same shade as her lipstick.

"You're Connor's sister?" she asks. "Damn. I expected someone weirder. Or louder."

"I'll take that as a compliment."

"Perfect. Sit. Drink. Tell us everything."

Connor disappears to the other end of the booth. I sit. The girls shift to make room like I've been part of this group for years.

And somehow, it's easy.

Lexi is sharp and warm. Maya says little, but every word matters. Rachel is chaos and doesn't even try to hide it—and it takes her maybe five minutes to let everyone know she's openly flirting with my brother.

It's kind of amazing watching him try to keep up.

She leans closer. He fumbles his drink. Then flexes like that makes it better.

"You okay there, goalie boy?" she asks.

"Totally fine," Connor says, voice cracking halfway through.

Carter leans toward me and mutters, "This is the worst seduction attempt I've ever seen."

"I'm right here!" Liam yells from across the table.

"You're always right here," Carter deadpans.

I laugh before I can stop myself. It feels... good. The kind of good that's easy to forget you missed.

Eventually, people drift. Lexi pulls Maya to the bar. Rachel drags Connor away—openly. Carter and Liam argue their way toward the dartboard. The table clears.

I find myself standing at the edge of the room, sipping the last of my drink. Trying not to think. Trying not to—

Ethan's next to me before I even notice.

"You good?"

"Define good."

He smiles, slow. "You didn't run. That's a win."

"The night's still young."

"You're good at this."

"At what?"

"Fitting in."

"Thanks. I'll list it as a marketable skill."

He nudges my arm with his shoulder, gentle. "Relax. I wasn't teasing."

"Could've fooled me."

"Okay," he says. "Maybe a little."

There's a pause. And I hate how comfortable it is.

I feel him more than I look at him. The heat of him. The space he takes up. The way he doesn't lean too close, but doesn't back off either.

Lexi's watching us. I know it without looking. I also know she's smirking.

I turn. Right into his chest.

His hand catches my elbow, firm and steady.

"Careful," he says, voice low. "Would hate for you to bruise something vital."

I glance up at him. "You planning to trip me?"

"No," he says. "You're just… distracting."

I roll my eyes. "That's a terrible line."

"You're still standing here."

"Give it another minute."

He grins. "Wanna go insult me some more over a few shots, my treat?"

I hesitate.

Then nod. "Lead the way."

The bar smells like sweat, lime, and bad decisions. Ethan orders tequila with that stupid, confident look like he knows what this is going to do to me.

He hands me a shot. Lime. Salt. The whole setup.

"To burying the hatchet," he says.

"We've had a few."

"Then here's to burying the biggest one."

I clink his glass. We throw them back.

It burns. But I want more.

The second shot goes down easier.

When I look at him, there's a softness in his face I didn't expect.

"Better?" he asks.

I nod. "Almost tolerable."

"Almost?"

"Let's not get carried away."

The music shifts. Deeper bass. Lights low and golden. Someone yells about the dance floor. I see hands, movement, energy. Then everyone's gone.

Ethan looks at me. Not asking. Not pressuring. Just waiting.

"Come on, entertain me for one dance," he says.

"Dancing isn't crossing one of your lines is it?"

He leans in just slightly. "One dance. Just for fun, as friends?"

It's a bad idea.

I do it anyway.

The floor pulses with heat. Ethan's hand finds my waist. My fingers touch his shoulder. We move, slow at first. He's smooth. Confident. His hand rests just low enough to be intentional.

"I thought you'd be worse at this," I murmur.

He grins. "You wound me."

"You'll live."

We fall into rhythm. I don't overthink it. I just move.

The music slows again. My hips roll. His breath catches. I don't stop.

His hand slides to my lower back, pulling me closer.

We don't talk. We don't look away.

The space between us disappears.

Chest to chest. Thigh to thigh.

And something about it feels dangerous. Too familiar.

"Still think I'm tolerable?" he asks.

"You're awful."

"You're into it."

I don't answer.

Not when my body's already answering for me.

His thigh slots between mine. I shift closer. His jaw flexes. His breath is on my cheek.

We keep moving.

One song becomes another.

And when we finally step apart, it's slower than it should be.

His hand brushes mine as he lets go.

And I hate that part of me misses the contact already.

Chapter 10

Avery

The night stretches.

One drink turns into three. Someone orders fries for the table, and half of them end up on the floor. Rachel's perched in Connor's lap now, drunk off her ass and aggressively explaining astrology while he pretends not to be in love, I have never seen him like this.

Carter is singing along to a song that's not playing. Liam is arm-wrestling a guy we don't know. Maya is sipping quietly and judging everyone from behind her glass like a benevolent wine deity.

And me?

I'm on my second wind, laughing too loud, cheeks flushed, body still humming from that dance with Ethan like the song hasn't stopped.

I haven't looked at him since.

Okay, I've looked once.

Fine. Twice.

And every time, he was already looking back.

Lexi leans over with the smirk of someone who absolutely knows something she shouldn't.

"You good?" she asks.

"Yeah," I say, voice lighter than I expect.

She taps her glass to mine. "You two look good when you let yourselves have fun."

I arch a brow. "You're being subtle and I hate it."

She shrugs. "Comes with age."

"You're literally two years older than me."

"And yet so wise."

"Theres nothing going on between us."

"Never say never."

And then she clinks her glass against mine and we drink.

Rachel tips sideways into Connor with a giggle-snort hybrid that could be used to summon demons.

Connor catches her with a hand to her back, brows up. "Whoa. You okay?"

"I'm fabulous," she says. "I'm also pretty sure I'm spinning."

Connor looks at Lexi. Then to me. Then back to Rachel, who's currently attempting to flirt with her own shoe.

"I should take her home," he says.

Rachel immediately perks up. "Ooooh, are you trying to get me to bed, goalie boy?"

Connor visibly short-circuits.

"I—what? No—I mean—just wanna make sure you get home okay."

Rachel grins, victorious. "My hero."

Lexi chokes on her drink. Maya is fully filming.

Connor stands, carefully guiding her up like he's handling a bomb with lipstick. "Ethan," he says over his shoulder, "can you make sure Avery gets home safe?"

I freeze.

Ethan looks up. Blinks once. "Yeah. Sure."

"Cool," Connor says. "Text when you're back?"

"Yup."

And just like that, it's just us.

Me. Him. And the after-hours glow of a night that's gone on too long and not long enough.

The city is quiet in that early-morning way—everything soft and silver, like the world's been dipped in moonlight and silence. The sidewalks are mostly empty. Just streetlights and the echo of our footsteps.

Ethan walks beside me. Not too close. Not far.

I steal a glance.

He looks... relaxed. Or trying to be.

"I had fun tonight," I say, finally.

"Me too."

We walk a few more paces.

"You look good tonight," he adds.

I glance at him. "Thank you."

"Are we friends now?"

I laugh, breath curling in the cold. "You always like this with your teammates' sisters?"

"Only the ones who almost drown me and look stupid hot in black dresses."

My pulse stutters. "You're drunk, again."

"I'm not. I sobered up somewhere between tequila and that last song."

"That's unfortunate."

"Why?"

"Because drunk Ethan's more fun."

The apartment door clicks shut behind us with a soft finality.

I should head to my room.

I should say goodnight.

Instead, I toe off my shoes in the entryway and pause, still facing the door, keys in my hand like I've forgotten how to move.

Ethan steps in behind me. Quiet. Heavy with unsaid things.

I glance over my shoulder. "You want water or something?"

He shrugs. "Sure."

We walk to the kitchen in silence. The lights are low—just the under-cabinet glow humming, making everything feel soft and not real. I grab two glasses, fill them, hand him one.

He watches me take a sip.

"You always stall when you don't want the night to end?" he asks.

I pause. "You always terrible at flirting when you're nervous?"

He leans against the counter. "I'm not nervous."

"Liar."

My breath catches. Not all at once—just a small hitch, like my body's catching up to where my mind refuses to go.

"Is this part of the hatchet-burying process?" I ask, my voice lower than I meant. "Because I'm not sure tequila and heavy eye contact counts as resolution."

"It's a start," he says, just above a whisper.

He takes a step closer.

I don't move.

His voice dips. "Tell me to stop if you don't want me to touch you. Because I really fucking want to touch you."

I should say something.

But I don't.

So he does.

His hand comes up, slow, measured. He tucks a strand of hair behind my ear, fingers brushing my skin like he's memorizing the shape of me. Just that small contact sends a shiver down my spine. My stomach tightens. My pulse climbs.

Then he leans in.

And he kisses me.

It starts slow. Deliberate. His lips part against mine, testing, waiting. I don't hesitate. I lean in, mouth meeting his with pressure that's anything but soft. It's hungry. Heated. But not rushed.

His tongue slides against mine, smooth and steady. No fumbling. No guessing. He kisses like he knows what he wants, like he's done thinking about it. His hand settles at the back of my neck, not tight, but firm—anchoring me there.

I kiss him back just as hard.

There's nothing timid in it now. My tongue meets his, mouths open wider, breaths sharper. His other hand finds my waist, fingers splaying just beneath the edge of my shirt. My stomach jumps under his touch, but I don't pull away. I let him feel me. Let him hold me.

My hand curls into the front of his shirt. I'm not sure if I'm holding him closer or holding myself together.

The kiss deepens—deeper than it should. His lips press harder. His tongue moves with mine like we're already too far in to stop now. My chest is tight, lungs barely catching air between passes, and still we don't break apart.

We've kissed before. But this is different.

He groans low in his throat, and that sound alone makes me want to do it again—deeper, harder, longer.

But I pull back first.

Breathing hard. Heart pounding.

We're both still too close.

Both staring.

Both completely wrecked.

"Shit," I whisper.

"Yeah," he breathes. His voice is gravel. "You have no idea what you're doing to me."

I smile, breathless. "I think I do."

He growls something half-incoherent and then his hands are on my dress—palms sliding up the back, fingers curling around the zipper.

He pauses.

I don't.

I reach behind me, pull it down myself.

It slips from my shoulders. Pools at my feet.

He goes very, very still.

Black lace.

My favorite set. Not because I thought this would happen—but because I wanted to feel powerful tonight. Sharp. Untouchable.

But the way he's looking at me now?

It's like he's *starving.*

His hands settle on my bare waist. "You're killing me."

"You'll survive."

"No. I really won't."

He dips his head and kisses down my neck, slow, reverent, all heat and patience.

My fingers find the hem of his shirt. I yank it up.

He lifts his arms so I can pull it off completely.

The second it hits the floor, I trace his chest with both hands—hard lines, warm skin, the slow thud of his heart beneath my palm.

"Jesus," I mutter. "What do you *do* in the gym, bench-press planets?"

He laughs, but it's cut off when I kiss him again.

Harder.

Deeper.

His hands find my thighs and suddenly I'm on the kitchen counter.

Dress somewhere on the floor. My legs around his hips. His mouth back on mine like he's forgotten the rest of the world exists.

His lips drag down my throat.

His hand palms my thigh, then drags up. Higher. *Almost.*

I gasp and he stills.

"You want me to stop?"

I don't even hesitate.

"No."

"Good girl."

His mouth is back on mine before I can catch my breath—hungry now, not just heat but *need*, like he's trying to kiss every moment we've avoided until now into submission.

His hands grip my thighs tighter, dragging me to the edge of the counter, pulling me into him so close I can't think straight.

When I moan—soft and involuntary—he makes a sound in the back of his throat that's downright feral.

"You're driving me insane," he mutters, voice wrecked. "I can't—God, I can't think when you look at me like that."

I don't say anything.

I don't need to.

Because then he's kissing down my jaw, over the hinge of it, dragging his mouth to my throat like he's mapping my pressure points by instinct.

A bite—soft, sharp—just above my collarbone.

I gasp again.

"Too much?" he asks, breath hot against my skin.

"Not enough."

His eyes flash dark.

And then he's lowering me—pushing me gently back so my spine hits the counter, my hands braced behind me, legs still wrapped around his hips.

His mouth trails lower. Kisses over the edge of my bra. Then lower. A kiss between my ribs. A warm, deliberate drag of lips down the center of my stomach.

I'm already trembling, trying not to fall apart just from the way he's taking his time. From the way his fingers knead into my thighs like he can't decide if he wants to hold me in place or worship me.

He glances up.

That look—messy, focused, completely undone—punches the breath out of my lungs. His mouth is red, eyes glazed like he's already drunk on me, and he hasn't even started yet.

"You're not real," he whispers, voice rough enough to scrape.

I laugh. It comes out breathy, wrecked already, because *I'm not okay*. Not when he's looking at me like that. Like I'm a secret he's dying to ruin.

He kisses just above the waistband of my panties, and my back arches instinctively, offering more. My fingers dive into his hair without permission, fisting in the strands like I need an anchor.

He groans when I pull. *God*, that sound.

He kisses my hip. Then bites. A sharp sting that makes my thighs jerk around his shoulders.

And that's the moment I realize:

This man is going to **ruin** me.

I swear I black out for a second.

Not from the alcohol. Not from the night. But from the way his mouth moves down my body like he's praying with his lips and sinning with his tongue.

His hands slide beneath my thighs, curling around to grip the backs of them, pulling me to the very edge of the counter like he's not risking anything—he *owns* it. He *owns me*. The cold granite at my back is nothing compared to the heat radiating from him.

I feel him everywhere.

His breath ghosting over my skin.

The scratch of his stubble against my belly.

His hands, large and rough, sliding up and down my thighs like he's trying to calm himself down—except it's not working.

"Ethan," I whisper. My voice cracks in the middle. Broken.

He pauses.

His lips are just above the line of my underwear now.

He groans—deep, guttural—and presses a kiss right there. Right over the thinnest scrap of lace between us.

Then he *bites.*

I gasp, loud, hands flying back to the counter to keep myself grounded, but it's no use—I'm already on fire.

He doesn't rush.

Oh no. He takes his goddamn time.

His tongue traces slow, maddening patterns over the lace—circles, lines, a soft flick that makes me sob. His fingers dig into my thighs, spreading me wider, holding me in place like I might escape. Like he'd never let me if I tried.

He alternates—feather light flicks with his tongue, then sudden heat and pressure that makes me grind against his mouth without meaning to. Every time I think I know what he's about to do, he shifts. Changes rhythm. Pulls back just to make me whimper and then dives in harder, deeper, rougher.

He's *studying* me.

Like this is science.

Like he's learning the exact pattern to unmake me molecule by molecule.

I whimper his name. I don't even mean to.

He groans in response and pulls my panties aside like he's done being polite.

And then—*then*—his mouth is on me.

No barrier. No pretense.

Just his tongue, hot and slick and sinful, sliding through my folds, licking me like I'm the sweetest thing he's ever tasted.

He moans against me and my hips buck. My whole body tightens.

His grip on my thighs turns bruising, holding me open while his tongue circles my clit, flicks it, *sucks it*, and I nearly scream. My fingers claw at his scalp, and he just moans again—deeper this time, like *he's* the one coming undone.

And I think I might. I think I really, truly might lose it on this fucking kitchen counter.

And then I fall off the edge, he keeps going and lets me ride out the pleasure. When he feels me relax he pulls back. Just enough to speak.

His voice is gravel and sex and pride.

"I've wanted to do that since you sat in my lap in the shower."

I look down at him.

And Jesus Christ, he looks *ruined*.

Lips slick with me, eyes blown wide, jaw tight like he's holding himself back with the thinnest thread of control. His chest rises and falls like he's been running. His hair's a mess from my hands, and his hands are still fisted around my thighs like he'll never let go.

And it's because of me.

I pull him up—urgent, greedy—mouth crashing into his like I need him to survive. The taste of me on his lips sends a thrill down my spine. I moan into him, nails raking down his back, and he groans, low and feral, as he grinds against me.

His hands slide up—over my ass, my hips—gripping so hard I know I'll feel it tomorrow, and I *want to.*

I hook my fingers in his waistband, tug.

"Bedroom?" I gasp.

He pauses—just for a second—and rests his forehead against mine, breath ragged.

"If I take you to bed right now," he says, voice shaking with restraint, "I'm not stopping."

I blink. My heart punches my ribs.

And I whisper, "I don't want you to stop."

He's breathing like he just lost a fight.

Like he already knows he's going to lose the next one, too.

He lifts me—arms under my thighs, hands gripping tight—and I wrap myself around him instinctively.

He carries me down the hall like it's nothing.

Like he's done it before in his head a hundred times.

His mouth doesn't leave mine, not even when he kicks the door open with one foot and walks us into the dark.

He sets me down like I'm something precious.

Then ruins that immediately by pushing me back onto the mattress.

I fall onto the bed, hair fanned out, skin flushed, completely undone—and still wanting more.

He stands at the edge, breathing hard, just looking at me.

The lace. The hair. The lips he's already kissed swollen.

"You're unreal," he murmurs.

"Get over here."

He chuckles, but it's low, wrecked. Then he's crawling over me—slow, deliberate, eyes locked on mine.

"Say it again," he says, mouth brushing my jaw. "That you want this."

"I want this."

He exhales like I just gave him permission to live.

His mouth finds mine again—rougher now, all tongue and need. His hands slide under me, lifting, shifting, grinding into me in a way that makes my entire body arch.

I gasp his name. He growls mine.

It's clumsy in the best way—hands everywhere, moans too loud, skin sliding against skin.

His mouth moves lower. Over my chest. Down my ribs. Across my stomach.

Every bite is a threat.

He hooks his fingers into the lace at my hips.

Pauses.

One last look.

One last question.

"Want me to stop?"

I shake my head. "If you stop, I swear I'll kill you."

His smile is pure sin.

And then?

He doesn't stop.

Chapter 11

Ethan

Her breath hitches.

It's quiet—barely a sound—but it slices through the air like a match strike. That tiny, involuntary gasp when my fingers graze the band of her panties?

That's it. That's the moment.

I don't ask again.

I don't have to.

Because I *know*.

I see it in her eyes—wide, dark, dilated with want.

I feel it in the way her hips lift—wordless, desperate, aching for more.

I hear it in every breath she lets out—ragged, sweet, like surrender.

So I take.

I hook my thumbs into the lace and slide her panties down her legs, slow and deliberate. My gaze never leaves hers as they drop to the floor, forgotten, unimportant.

Because the only thing that matters now is *her*—laid out, trembling, mine.

I stay between her legs, kneeling, palms braced on her thighs. Her skin is hot under my touch, goosebumps racing ahead of my fingers. I press my mouth to her inner thigh, open-mouthed, teeth dragging lightly across her skin. She jerks, gasping, already unraveling.

I tease her first.

One finger sliding through her slick folds, slow, lazy, spreading her open for me. She whines—high, breathless—hips lifting instinctively.

"Look at you," I murmur against her skin. "So fucking wet, and I haven't even—"

She cuts me off with a strangled moan as I push two fingers inside her—deep, slow, curling just right—and press my thumb against her clit at the same time. Her body jerks. Her thighs tighten around my hand. She's panting now, eyes rolling back as I work her with calculated precision, every movement designed to make her fall apart.

But I don't let her come.

I stop right at the edge—pulling back, withdrawing my fingers, watching her blink up at me in disbelief, lips parted and trembling.

"Ethan..." she breathes.

I rise, towering over her, my body between her thighs and my hand fisted around myself now, already so hard it hurts. I drag the head of my cock through her slick heat, just once, slow and deliberate, and her whole body arches off the bed.

"Is this what you want?" I ask, voice low, almost a growl.

She nods—frantic. "Yes. Please."

"Beg me."

She swallows hard, cheeks flushed, eyes wild. And then she says it, voice cracking like glass:

"Please, Ethan. I need you."

That's it. That's the moment I snap.

I thrust into her with one deep, possessive stroke, burying myself to the hilt, and she cries out—a strangled, broken sound like she's been hit with something holy.

"F-fuck," she gasps. "Oh my God—"

I give her no time to adjust. No pause. No mercy.

I grip her thighs and fuck into her hard, each thrust deep and bruising, every inch a claim. She meets me stroke for stroke, her legs wrapping around my waist, pulling me closer, tighter, *deeper*. Her nails rake down my back—sharp, stinging—and I welcome the pain.

I want it.

I want *all* of it.

The moans. The sweat. The frantic grind of hips and skin. The way her voice breaks when she says my name like it's the only word she remembers.

"Ethan—fuck—don't stop—"

I don't.

Because this isn't just about getting off. It's about *owning* every inch of her. About showing her what it means to be mine.

Her hands are in my hair, pulling, anchoring herself to me. Her chest presses against mine, damp with sweat and arousal, and I kiss her—hard and messy and open-mouthed—like I want to crawl inside her and never leave.

"I want you to feel this tomorrow," I growl into her ear. "I want you limping when you walk. I want you to remember exactly what I did to you every time you close your eyes."

She chokes on a moan, back arching, thighs trembling.

She's close. I feel it. Every muscle in her body goes tight, her breathing shallow and desperate.

"Come for me," I command.

And she does—with a cry so raw it damn near undoes me. Her whole body clenches, legs shaking, her walls pulsing around me as she falls apart beneath me.

I keep going.

Chasing the high.

Losing myself in her.

My thrusts grow rougher, sloppier, until I feel the edge barreling toward me and I snap—buried deep, body shaking, coming with a groan ripped from the pit of my fucking soul.

We stay like that for a second—panting, tangled, wrecked.

Her body beneath mine, trembling. Her hands in my hair. My face in her neck. Our hearts pounding in the same shattered rhythm.

And in that moment, I know I've fucked up.

Because this?

This wasn't just sex.

Chapter 12

Avery

I wake up sore just like he promised.

And not in a "slept weird" kind of way. No, this is the kind of sore that comes with a warning label and a very smug hockey player somewhere in the apartment.

My legs ache in places that haven't been properly exercised since before the scandal, and my throat? Dry. From the moaning. Obviously.

I don't open my eyes right away.

Because if I do, I'll have to look at the man currently half-draped over me, arm heavy on my waist, breath warm against my neck like he belongs there. Like this is normal.

It's not.

We had sex.

Amazing, soul-shattering, Olympic-level sex. On a kitchen counter. In a bed. On top of the metaphorical grave we just dug for our emotional boundaries.

And now I'm lying here, naked and stupid and very aware of how *not okay* this is.

Ethan stirs behind me, shifts slightly. His hand slides up my ribs like he's done it before. Like this isn't new.

I open my mouth to speak. To say something clever, maybe sarcastic.

What comes out is:

"This can't happen again."

His hand stills.

A pause.

Then, "Yeah."

I shift to sit up, dragging the sheet with me, even though modesty is long gone and buried under a pile of regret and lace.

"We were drunk," I say, reaching for logic like it's going to save me. "Tired. Emotionally compromised. Again."

He props himself up on one elbow, hair a mess, eyes still heavy with sleep and sin. "Right."

"We shouldn't have—"

"Yeah," he cuts in, voice quieter now. "I know."

Silence stretches between us like a wire.

I stand. Find my robe. Wrap it around myself.

He doesn't move. Just watches me like I'm a dream he accidentally touched.

"We're living together," I say, more to myself than him. "We have to be... smart."

Ethan nods slowly. "Totally."

"We're roommates. That's it."

"Exactly."

I meet his eyes.

Neither of us believes a damn word we just said.

And we both know it.

Chapter 13

Ethan

The thing about hockey is: it never waits.

It doesn't care that your personal life is a wreck. It doesn't care if you haven't slept properly in days or if the girl you definitely weren't supposed to sleep with keeps walking around the apartment in tiny shorts and zero shame. The puck drops when it drops.

And right now? We're twenty-four hours out from our first game of the season, and Dad is already yelling like we've lost.

"Wilson! Pick up your goddamn stick and skate like your contract depends on it!"

I mutter something under my breath and push off harder, slicing across the ice, breath fogging in the cold, thighs burning in the best way. At least when I'm here—on the ice, in motion—I can forget.

Mostly.

The guys are amped today. Practice is loud, aggressive, all chirps and chaos.

Liam's already tried to body check me twice, which is his way of saying *I love you*, and Carter's skating backwards while yelling something about his "emotional support jockstrap" needing retirement.

Classic.

"Yo," Liam calls out as we break into drills, skating up beside me. "So, speaking of retirement, anyone know what the hell happened with Connor and Rachel last weekend? Dude looked like he was ready to propose or combust."

Carter skates up too, grinning like the devil. "Yeah, did we miss something? Did the goalie finally get laid?"

Connor, ahead of us, slows down just enough to hear.

"Nothing happened," he says flatly, not looking back.

"Oh come on," Carter groans. "She was *in your lap*, man."

Connor doesn't flinch. "She was drunk. I got her home."

"That's what I said after prom junior year," Liam snorts.

Connor stops skating.

Turns.

And *glares*.

"Let it go."

Liam raises his hands like he's just been caught shoplifting feelings. "Damn, bro. Didn't know you was *that* sensitive."

"Nothing happened," Connor says again, voice hard.

The group mutters and shifts, a few guys backing off, sensing the line.

"Did you see how hot Avery looked, if I'd known his sister looked like *that*," Carter says casually, "I might've volunteered to be the one getting her home."

The air shifts.

Everyone laughs—until Connor spins.

Fast.

He's *in Carter's face* before I can blink, shoving him back with one hand to the chest.

"Don't. Talk. About my sister."

Carter's eyes go wide. "Whoa—dude, chill."

Connor doesn't move. "Not a fucking word. From any of you. Got it?"

Dead silence.

Coach's whistle blows from the other end of the ice, but no one moves. We're all watching the stand-off like it's about to turn into a heavyweight title fight.

Liam mutters, "Jesus. Protective much?"

"She's not a joke," Connor snaps. "She's not a party story. And if I hear anyone say shit like that again, I'll break your jaw in the locker room."

Carter raises both hands, still backing off. "Message received, goalie."

Connor turns and skates away without another word.

And I?

I am in full *panic mode* inside.

Because if that's his reaction to a *joke*—and he doesn't even know what *actually* happened?

Yeah.

I'm fucked.

The locker room clears out slowly.

Carter slinks out first, still looking mildly traumatized, followed by Liam who's already retelling the "Connor threatened homicide for sister jokes" saga like it's a bedtime story. The rest of the guys trail out one by one, dragging duffel bags and sweat in equal measure.

I hang back.

Not on purpose.

I'm just slow today. Mind tangled. Muscles tighter than they should be. I towel off, sit there in half my gear, and try to think about anything *other* than how close I came to full cardiac arrest when someone called Avery hot out loud.

The door creaks open again, and I glance up—expecting Connor, ready to pretend I wasn't rethinking every life decision I've ever made.

But it's not Connor.

It's my dad.

Coach Volkov now. Or just... James, I guess. Depends on the room.

He leans against the doorway, arms crossed, still wearing his team jacket like he was born in it. His eyes sweep the empty room, then land on me.

"Everyone survive the testosterone convention?"

I snort. "Barely. Connor almost broke Carter's nose."

James raises an eyebrow. "Was it justified?"

I smirk. "Carter made a joke about his sister."

A knowing nod. "Fair."

He walks in, grabs the bench across from mine, and sits. No clipboard. No authority. Just... Dad.

And that still feels weird, sometimes. Good. But weird.

"You alright?" he asks.

I nod. "Yeah."

"You don't look alright."

I laugh. "I never look alright. That's just my face."

He gives me that half-smile that still feels new—like it's not just for show anymore. "I mean it. I've been watching you. You're skating hard. Focused. Pissed off, but dialed in. You okay?"

"Yeah," I say after a second. "I'm good. Just... tired. Lot going on."

"Anything I should know about?"

"Like what?"

"Like whatever has you looking worse than normal. I thought you were on track for a good season this year, unless there's something else going on, you should be on cloud nine."

I shrug. "It's just the season. The pressure. And, uh... my living situation's been interesting."

That earns a sharper look.

"Interesting how?"

"Just... lots going on. Hard to think. And trying to find a new place."

He nods. "Yeah. Things okay with Connor?"

"Yeah. He's a good dude."

"And his sister, Avery is it?"

My spine locks.

He says her name casually. Too casually.

"Why?" I ask, trying not to sound like I just swallowed a live wire.

James shrugs. "Connor mentioned she's back in town. Said she's staying at his for a while as well."

I nod slowly. "She is."

"She doing okay?"

I stare at him.

"She's figuring things out. Rough year."

He hums. "Aren't we all. Well if it gets too much there, you're welcome to come stay at mine."

"You mean yours and Lexi's? I am happy for you both, truly, but I don't need to see it first hand thanks dad."

A pause. The room quiets, save for the hum of the lights and the sound of my own heartbeat trying to punch its way out of my chest.

"I'm proud of you, you know," he says.

That stops me cold.

I look up. "What?"

"We've come a long way in the last year, I think things are looking good for us."

My chest tightens.

"I'm still a mess," I say, quietly.

"So was I," he replies. "Still am. But we're working on it."

Another pause.

Then, "You ever need to talk—about anything—you know I'm around, right?"

I nod. Swallow hard. "Yeah. Thanks."

He stands, gives me one last look.

Then says, "Tell Connor breaking jaws are not worth the suspension. But I respect the energy."

And then he's gone.

And I sit there, towel around my neck, hands clenched on my knees, heart full of way too many things I'm not ready to unpack.

Because my dad's proud of me.

Because Avery's off-limits.

Because Connor's already one bad joke away from a prison sentence.

And because the only thing I want right now is to go home...

...and see her.

Chapter 14

Avery

I am not thinking about him.

I'm not.

I'm eating cold leftover pasta straight from the container, curled up on Connor's too-perfect designer couch in socks that could double as blankets, with a clay mask cracking down my cheekbones like dry earth, and I am absolutely not thinking about Ethan Wilson.

My phone buzzes.

Mia:

How's living with Hot Mess Express?

Me:

Fine.

Normal.

Totally non-life-ruining.

Mia:

That's the exact tone people use when they're lying to the FBI.

Me:

It's chill. I'm chill. Everything is chill.

Mia:

Girl. What happened?

Me:

We had sex.

Mia:

You had SEX with your brother's best friend in his apartment?

Me:

Correction: he started it on the counter. He finished it in his bed. I was simply a passenger.

Mia:

A very naked, very willing passenger? OH MY GOD!

Me:

Shut up.

Mia:

So was it just hot, or hot and emotionally destabilizing?

Me:

...Both.

Mia:

So you saw God.

Me:

I saw something.

Mia:

And now you're what?

Me:

I am nurturing my body post-trauma.

Mia:

Oh my god, he rearranged you.

Me:

Mentally. Physically. Spiritually.

Mia:

I'm so proud. But also horrified.

Me:

You should be. It was a bad decision.

Mia:

And yet you'd do it again if he looked at you the same way.

I don't answer that one.

Mia:

Avery. You're typing. And then you stop. That's guilt. That's post-destruction hesitation.

Me:

He's Connor's best friend.

Mia:

And you're Connor's adult sister. Not a nun. Or a paper doll. Or a contract clause.

Me:

This isn't normal.

Mia:

You're not normal. That's why I like you.

Me:

I can't go there again. Not after what happened.

Mia:

What happened? Besides the emotionally loaded, blackout-worthy orgasm in the bed of a man you swore you hated?

Me:

He didn't look at me weird the next morning.

Mia:

What do you mean?

Me:

He didn't look at me like I was a mistake. Or a regret. He was just... normal. Too normal.

Mia:

Oof. That's worse. That means it probably meant something and he doesn't know what to do with it.

Me:

I don't want it to mean something.

Mia:

Liar.

Me:
You're the worst.
Mia:
And yet here I am. Talking you through your sex-fueled emotional collapse like a true best friend.

I toss the phone onto the other end of the couch and groan into a throw pillow.

I am absolutely, one hundred percent—

Thinking about him.

I sigh and shove another forkful of pasta in my mouth.

He's been quiet the last few days. Focused. Out early, back late, all sharp edges and sweat and eyes that barely meet mine. Like he didn't see me naked and say things that haven't left my bloodstream since.

It's fine.

It's better this way.

I need space. He needs focus. Everything is under control.

Then the door opens.

And just like that, *control* packs its bags and flips me off on the way out.

Ethan walks in wearing joggers, a team hoodie, and a towel slung around his neck like he just got done starring in a Gatorade commercial designed to personally ruin me.

His hair is damp. His shirt clings in all the worst-best ways. And his jawline?

Offensive.

I blink. Swallow my pasta. Immediately regret everything.

"Hey," he says, voice rough like he's been yelling over drills all day.

"Hey," I manage, through a mouthful of carbs and shame.

He drops his bag by the door, stretches like a Greek tragedy with biceps, and walks toward the kitchen.

"How was practice?" I ask, aiming for casual and landing somewhere near *suspiciously breathy*.

He shrugs, grabs a water from the fridge. "Fine. Tense. Coach yelled. Connor almost committed manslaughter."

I raise an eyebrow. "Why?"

"Someone made a joke about you."

Oh. "Me?"

"Yeah. Carter said something dumb. Connor nearly threw him through the glass."

My stomach flips. "What did he say?"

Ethan takes a long sip of water. His jaw tightens.

"That you were hot."

My brain short-circuits.

"And... Connor freaked out?"

"Like full rage blackout. Told everyone you're off-limits and threatened to break jaws." He glances at me then, expression unreadable. "Nobody's saying anything now."

I snort. "He's so dramatic."

Ethan smiles faintly. "It was kind of impressive."

I lean back into the couch, trying to act like my heart isn't doing Olympic-level flips.

"And you?" I ask.

"Me?"

"Did you say anything?"

He tilts his head, eyes darkening just slightly.

"I didn't have to."

Silence settles. Tense. Electric. The kind that hums under your skin.

I break it first.

"Well. Good to know I have a human guard dog in goalie pads."

Ethan laughs, then leans against the counter, watching me.

"You know," he says, "we never actually said what that night meant."

I blink.

"Which night?"

He raises an eyebrow. "Avery."

I stare at him, fork halfway to my mouth.

Oh.

That night.

I swallow.

"I thought we agreed it was a one-time thing. A bad idea. A lapse in judgment."

He nods slowly. "Right. Totally. Thing is I've been thinking about it ever since."

My pulse stutters.

"That sounds like a *you* problem," I say, forcing a smirk.

He walks toward me. Slow. Intentional.

And suddenly I'm not smirking anymore.

He stops in front of the couch, towel still draped around his neck, eyes locked on mine like he's trying to figure out if I'm bluffing.

"Yeah," he murmurs, voice low. "But I think it's about to be *our* problem again."

The words are still hanging in the air when Ethan moves.

One step.

Two.

Then his hand is on my wrist—firm but careful—and he's pulling me up off the couch.

I barely have time to blink before my back hits the wall behind me.

Hard.

Not enough to hurt.

Just enough to make me gasp.

He cages me in with both arms, hands braced on either side of my head, body flush against mine, every inch of him radiating heat and hunger and pure, unfiltered *intention.*

"I thought we had rules," I whisper, because it's the only sentence I can find.

His eyes burn. "Screw the rules."

"Connor—"

"—is out for drinks," Ethan cuts in. "Told me he wouldn't be back until late."

His hand slides down the wall, grazing my waist.

"We've got hours."

I suck in a breath, heart stuttering like a trapped animal. "This is a bad idea."

"The best ones always are."

Then his mouth crashes into mine, and it's *done.*

The kiss is all teeth and tongue and pent-up fury disguised as need. His hands grab my hips, yank me forward into him like he's been waiting *days* to feel me again.

I moan—quiet, desperate—and he swallows it like it's his goddamn right.

"I've been thinking about this every second since the other night," he mutters against my mouth, his hand slipping under my shirt.

"You're insane," I breathe, fingers already fisting in his hoodie.

"You're no better," he growls, lifting me like I weigh nothing, wrapping my legs around his waist.

The world tilts as he pins me harder against the wall, hips grinding into mine, making me gasp as the friction sets every nerve on fire.

My hands tug at his shirt. "Take this off."

He obliges—pulling back just long enough to yank it over his head and drop it to the floor. Then he's on me again, mouth on my neck, biting, sucking, marking like he *wants me bruised.*

"You're playing with fire," I whisper, even as my hips grind down against him, chasing heat like a sinner at confession.

He smirks against my collarbone. "Then burn with me."

His fingers slide under the waistband of my shorts—no hesitation now—and I let out a choked sound as he drags them down just enough to touch me.

"You're soaked," he murmurs, voice wrecked. "Jesus, Avery."

"This is your fault," I hiss.

"I know," he says. "And I'm not sorry."

Then his fingers slide into me—deep and smooth—and I bite down on his shoulder to keep from crying out.

He moves like he remembers exactly how to break me apart. Like he's memorized every sound I make and wants to hear them *all.*

I moan instead—loud and unfiltered—and he groans, dropping his head to my shoulder, thrusting his fingers faster.

"You're gonna make me lose my mind," he growls.

"Good," I gasp. "Lose it. I'm already gone."

He pulls his fingers out, lifts me higher against the wall, one hand fisting in my hair now, the other dragging his sweats down just enough to free himself.

"Tell me to stop," he says again, voice shaking with restraint.

I wrap my arms around his neck, eyes locked on his. "Don't you dare."

And then he's inside me.

One hard thrust.

Deep. Hot. *Devastating.*

I cry out—soft, breathy, broken—and he swears under his breath like he's not going to survive this.

"Fuck, Avery—" he groans, slamming into me again. "You feel—Jesus—better than I remember."

I grip his shoulders, nails digging in. "Harder."

He growls.

And obeys.

The wall shakes behind us as he thrusts harder, faster, every movement dragging another sound out of me. I'm clinging to him like he's the only solid thing in the world. And he is. Right now, he *is.*

"You gonna come for me again?" he mutters, voice pure sin.

I can't even speak—I just nod, panting, whining, head falling back.

He thrusts deep—again and again—and then he shifts slightly, angling up, hitting that spot that makes my whole body seize.

"Oh my *God*—"

"There," he says, voice hoarse. "Right there?"

"YES—"

He doesn't stop.

And when I come—loud, messy, full-body—I collapse against him, nails raking down his back as I fall apart with his name on my lips.

He keeps going.

Fucking me through it.

Until he finally lets go—groaning into my neck, hips jerking as he comes deep inside me, breathing like he just survived war.

For a second, we don't move.

Just pant. Hold each other.

Feel everything.

Then he presses his forehead to mine, eyes still closed.

"Still think it's a bad idea?" he murmurs.

I smile.

And kiss him again.

Chapter 15

Avery

I wasn't planning to wear his number.

Okay, that's a lie.

I tried *not* to plan it. Swore I'd just wear black and stay invisible, clap politely when he scored and pretend I wasn't having full-body flashbacks to getting railed against a wall by the man currently listed as my "roommate."

But then Mia showed up.

And everything went to hell.

"Wait," she says, halfway through raiding my half-unpacked suitcase. "You're telling me you slept with him *again*, and you weren't planning to wear his number to the season opener?"

"I didn't *sleep* with him," I protest.

Mia raises an eyebrow. "Did you fall asleep in the same bed after he turned your spine into spaghetti?"

"...that's irrelevant."

"That's a yes. Put the damn jersey on."

"It's not even a jersey," I argue. "It's just a hoodie with his number on the back."

"Which is worse," she says, smug. "Because it's casual. Domestic. Suggestive of *ownership.* Connor's going to lose his mind."

"I don't care," I lie.

Mia tosses it at me. "Good. Then put it on."

Fifteen minutes later, I'm in the backseat of an Uber with Lexi, Maya, Rachel, and Mia, all looking like the cover of Sports Illustrated: Chaos Edition. Lexi's in a fitted blazer, Maya's sipping iced coffee like she's here to judge and journal about it, Rachel is in a crop top that says **PUCK YOU**, and Mia? Mia is in heels and ready to emotionally tackle someone.

"I cannot believe I'm finally meeting the infamous Wilson," she says, applying lip gloss like it's a weapon. "If he doesn't look wrecked from your vibes alone, I'll be disappointed."

"Can we *not* say 'wrecked'?" I mutter.

Lexi leans over. "So... you're really wearing his number, huh?"

I glance down at the black hoodie. The white **#21** stitched on the back.

My face warms. "It's just a hoodie."

Rachel cackles. "That's not *just* a hoodie. That's a post-coital power move disguised as fan merch."

"You guys are insufferable."

"You love it," Maya says calmly. "Besides, it's better than the time Lexi showed up in James's old practice jersey and got mistaken for his wife before they were even official."

Lexi waves a hand. "Tragic but effective."

The arena is already buzzing when we arrive. Fans everywhere. Kids with foam fingers. Couples in matching jerseys. The energy is electric—hopeful, hyped, *loud.*

We push through the chaos and find our seats—front row behind the glass, courtesy of Connor, who "just wanted us to have a good view." He has *no idea* what's about to hit him.

And then the players skate out.

The crowd *explodes.*

I find him instantly.

Ethan.

Number 21.

He's fast, sharp, focused—the way he always is on the ice. But then he slows for just a second, glancing up into the stands.

And he sees me.

His eyes lock on the hoodie.

His smirk could melt glaciers.

Mia leans over, whispering, "You are *so* getting laid after this game."

Rachel's too busy screaming Connor's name to notice the look *he* gives me next.

Because Connor sees me too.

And stops skating.

Just for a beat.

Eyes on the hoodie.

On the number.

And then they narrow.

Lexi mutters, "Oh no."

Maya sips her coffee. "Oh yes."

Connor glares up at me.

Mouths something.

"What are you wearing?"

Not "hi," not "thanks for coming," not "good to see you."

Just pure, unfiltered, *big brother panic.*

And then the puck drops.

And the game begins.

And so does the absolute unraveling of my life.

Ethan Wilson is *on fire.*

The puck barely hits the ice before he's chasing it down like he's got vengeance in his skates. First period? He scores. Second period? Two assists and a hit so brutal the guy had to recalibrate his soul on the bench.

By the third?

He's electric.

Fast, sharp, cocky in a way that has the whole arena on edge—fans screaming, kids banging on the glass, and *me* clenching the railing like it's the only thing keeping me upright.

"He's different tonight," Maya murmurs, watching intently.

"Dialed in," Lexi says, nodding. "Focused."

Rachel whistles. "Jesus. That man is skating like he's trying to make up for every single bad headline he's ever had."

"I mean," Mia says casually, "he *is* getting laid now."

I elbow her hard.

"Oh, relax," she grins. "If he keeps playing like this, I say we encourage it."

On the ice, Ethan takes a hit against the boards, recovers like nothing happened, and launches the puck down the rink with the kind of precision that has *both* commentators groaning.

"Wilson again—unbelievable stamina tonight. That's his third line shift without dropping pace."

"He's clearly out to prove something. Rumors swirled last season, but this guy? This version of Ethan Wilson? He's all business."

"Interesting note—we haven't seen him with anyone publicly for over a month now. No distractions, no off-ice drama. Looks like the Wilson comeback tour is in full swing."

I choke on my drink.

Mia looks at me like she wants to frame my expression.

"No distractions, huh?" she smirks.

"I hate everyone."

Lexi leans over, eyes twinkling. "You sure? Because he keeps looking up at our section."

I glance over.

Ethan is coasting past the bench after another clean assist, sweat dripping down his neck, smirk *dangerously illegal*, and yeah—his eyes flick to the glass.

Right to me.

The smile is subtle.

But it's there, and then he winks.

Rachel gasps. "He did *not*—"

"He did," Maya confirms, sipping her wine. "And honestly? I respect it."

Connor, down on the ice, doesn't see it.

Yet.

But the way Ethan is moving—like every goal is a middle finger to everyone who ever doubted him?

It's magnetic.

And I'm not the only one noticing.

A group of girls near the lower section are clearly plotting how to climb over the plexiglass. A reporter in the press box is already jotting down stats with a giddy expression. Even the opposing team is starting to hesitate when he hits the ice.

He's commanding. Unapologetic. Back from the edge and playing like he never left.

And the only thought echoing in my head?

Hes coming home with me, not any of the other girls here.

Not to the crowd. Not to the noise.

To *me*.

Game ends 4–2.

The fans erupt.

The players flood the bench.

And I sit there, heart thudding, hoodie warm around me, trying to remember what breathing felt like *before* I knew what it felt like to be looked at like that.

The bar is loud. Too loud.

Every surface is sticky, someone's already ordered three rounds of celebratory shots, and Liam is singing *We Are the Champions* with the passion of a drunk opera singer.

I should be thrilled.

And I *am*.

Mostly.

Because Ethan scored. The team won. Everyone's laughing, toasting, and pretending like the season hasn't even started grinding them down yet. It's all adrenaline and high-fives and "Did you *see* that pass?" on repeat.

But I also have Connor storming toward me like a man on a mission.

I brace.

He stops in front of me, arms crossed, face the exact shade of *big brother suspicion*.

"What," he says, eyes flicking to the hoodie I haven't taken off all night, "are you wearing?"

I blink innocently. "A hoodie."

He narrows his eyes. "Try again."

I glance down. Black. Oversized. Cozy. **#21.**

I shrug. "It's Ethan's. I was cold."

Connor glares. "That doesn't answer my question."

Lexi, bless her chaotic heart, appears beside me holding a vodka cranberry. "She was showing team spirit," she says sweetly. "And technically, she *was* warm, so it worked."

"Not helping," Connor mutters.

Maya chimes in from behind her glass of wine. "It's a peace offering."

"What?" Connor frowns.

I turn to him. "We've... made friends," I say, careful. Casual. Like I haven't been slammed against a wall by said friend in the last 48 hours. "Things were weird after I first got here. He was kind of a disaster, I was kind of... not nice."

"You threatened to leave him in the shower," Maya adds.

"I was being practical," I say.

Rachel grins. "She undressed him."

Connor chokes. "I'm sorry—none of this is helping!" He stares at me, and I can see the wheels turning.

"He's my teammate," he says slowly. "My best friend."

"And I'm your sister," I reply calmly. "Which is why I'm telling you the truth. We're friends now. That's all."

He frowns. "Since when?"

"Since I stopped hating him," I say, sipping my drink.

Connor still looks like he's trying to connect dots that absolutely do not add up.

"Seriously. He's just... been better lately. And I figured I'd show some support."

His eyes narrow again. "So the number on your back is just..."

"Friendly morale boosting," I say, deadpan. "Would you rather I wore yours?"

He looks horrified. "Absolutely not."

"Then shut up and let me support the team in peace."

There's a beat of silence.

Then—"Fine," he mutters, clearly not buying it. "But if I find out he laid a finger on you—"

"He'll be dead. Got it," I finish for him.

Connor grunts and stomps off to the bar, where Rachel immediately starts poking at him like she *enjoys* watching his blood pressure spike.

Behind me, Lexi snorts.

"Friends, huh?"

"Shut up," I mutter.

Across the room, Ethan catches my eye.

Raises his glass.

Smirks.

I look away before my face gives me away.

Again.

I make it exactly twelve feet out the bar's back door before I exhale like I've been holding my breath all night.

Because I have.

The noise, the crowd, the carefully measured banter with Connor—it was all a performance. Smile, sip, deflect. Act like Ethan's number on my back doesn't feel like a claim. Like his eyes didn't find mine every time something happened on the ice.

I just needed a minute.

One quiet second to reset. Breathe. Maybe Uber the hell home before I accidentally kiss him in front of half the team and my brother files for emotional custody.

But the universe, as usual, has other plans.

Because he's already outside.

Leaning against the brick wall, hoodie pushed up to his elbows, hair a mess, beer in hand. Looking like sin with a side of sweat and victory.

His eyes meet mine like he knew I'd come out here.

And suddenly I'm the one who can't breathe.

"Leaving without saying good game?" he asks, voice low.

I stop.

"You seemed busy," I reply, aiming for flippant.

He pushes off the wall, takes a step closer. "Wasn't that busy."

"You were the MVP," I say, arms crossed, heart racing. "I figured you'd be swarmed."

"I was," he says. "Didn't want them."

I raise a brow. "And what did you want?"

He doesn't answer right away.

Just takes a slow sip of his drink.

Then, softly—"*You.*"

The word hits low. Warm. Dangerous.

My stomach flips. "Ethan—"

"You wore my number."

"It was a hoodie."

"You wore *my number*," he repeats, stepping closer now. "In front of everyone. In front of your brother."

I swallow. "We said we'd be careful."

"You said that," he says. "I just nodded while I watched you walk around the apartment half-dressed."

"This isn't smart."

"I'm not trying to be smart," he murmurs. "I'm trying to be honest."

He's close now.

Too close.

I can smell the heat off his skin, the sharp edge of sweat and beer and whatever he's feeling that makes the space between us *hum.*

I glance toward the door.

It's cracked open. Voices drift out.

"Someone could come out here," I whisper.

"I don't care."

"You should."

"I don't."

My back hits the wall.

He cages me in—one hand next to my head, the other still holding his beer. But his eyes are only on me.

"I haven't stopped thinking about you," he says, voice low. Raw. "Not since that first night. Not since the shower. Not since the kitchen. Every time I close my eyes, it's you."

My pulse skitters. "You're not making this easy."

He leans in, just a breath away.

"I'm not trying to."

We don't kiss.

Not this time.

But it's closer than close.

And when his hand brushes mine—just barely—my whole body sparks.

I pull away first.

Barely.

"I have to go," I whisper.

He lets me.

But not before he murmurs, "Come home with me."

My breath catches.

"Just to sleep," he adds, eyes unreadable. "I won't touch you. Not unless you want me to."

I stare at him, because we live in the same apartment so of course we are going home together, but that's not what he meant.

And then I walk away.

Because if I stay?

I *will* kiss him.

And I'm not ready to admit I already feel owned.

Chapter 16

Avery

By the time I get back inside, the bar's even louder.

The guys are at one end, the girls at the other, and the music is just a little too bass-heavy for my current emotional stability. But I slide into the booth beside Lexi and act like my heart isn't still hammering against my ribs from *whatever that was* outside.

Lexi leans over. "You okay?"

"Peachy."

Rachel raises a brow. "You've got that 'I almost made a mistake I'd enjoy' look again."

"I'm fine."

Mia snorts. "You're spiralling. That's not fine. That's pre-murder tension."

"I just need a drink," I mutter, scanning the room—and then I see him.

Ethan.

At the bar.

Still in his hoodie, beer in hand, sweat-damp hair pushed back like he owns the place.

And beside him?

Two girls.

Leggy. Glossy. One in a crop top that looks like it was taxidermied off a Barbie. The other's got her hand on his arm, leaning in like she's auditioning for a role called *"I'm not subtle and I've never heard of shame."*

He doesn't pull away.

He doesn't engage either, to be fair—but he doesn't exactly look like he's in distress.

Something in me flares.

I look away fast. Back to my drink. Back to the table. Back to pretending I'm not two seconds from setting off the internal sprinkler system with jealousy-induced rage.

Rachel notices instantly.

"Ohhhh no," she says, grinning. "Don't look now—Barbie and Bratz just found themselves a Wilson."

Mia leans over. "That one's touching his bicep. She's got less shame than a reality TV contestant."

"Do I need to throw hands?" Rachel offers, cracking her knuckles with the enthusiasm of someone who *lives* for a bar brawl. "Because I *will*."

"No," I say tightly. "It's fine."

Lexi studies me. "You sure? Because you look like you're mentally flipping a table."

"I don't care," I lie, sipping my drink so hard I almost drown.

"Right," Maya says calmly. "That's why you're gripping the glass like it owes you rent."

I glance up again—stupid, stupid instinct—and this time Barbie leans into Ethan's ear.

And *he laughs.*

I see red.

Actual red.

"I hate her," I mutter under my breath.

"She's got clip-in extensions and delusions of relevance," Mia says. "You could take her."

"I'm not going to fight someone."

"Coward."

Lexi leans back. "Want me to go interrupt?"

"No."

"You sure?"

"YES."

I grit my teeth and turn away.

And I don't look again.

I *won't*.

...Until Ethan looks over at me.

Eyes locked.

Expression unreadable.

And slowly—subtly—he steps out of reach of the Barbie twins, says something to Liam, and starts walking toward me.

Rachel whistles. "Oh *shit*."

Lexi lifts her glass. "Showtime."

And I suddenly forget how to breathe.

I try not to look up, try to pretend I don't care, but I see the way Mia nudges Lexi and Rachel straightens like she's about to witness a crime of the heart.

Then he's there.

"Hey," Ethan says, voice low and unreadable. "Can I steal you for a sec?"

Rachel immediately makes a strangled *choking back a cackle* sound.

Lexi covers her smile with her glass.

I sigh, trying to keep my face neutral, and slide out of the booth.

He leads me a few steps away, not far—just enough to duck into the edge of the hallway where it's quieter, darker, more... *dangerous.*

He stops. Turns.

And *stares.*

"What?" I say, crossing my arms, trying to seem unbothered.

He raises a brow. "So we're doing this now?"

"Doing what?"

"The pretending thing."

I blink. "You're going to have to be more specific."

His jaw ticks. "You were jealous."

"I was not."

He leans in. "You glared at that girl like you were going to murder her with a napkin."

"She had her hand on your arm," I snap before I can stop myself.

His mouth twitches—somewhere between a smirk and a sigh. "And you *hated* it."

"I didn't hate it," I say. "I just thought it was gross."

Ethan steps closer, just a fraction, but it's enough to short-circuit every nerve in my body.

"Say it."

"Say what?"

"That you didn't like her touching me."

I swallow. "You're making this weird."

"No," he says, voice softer now. Lower. "You're just mad I let her get close."

"I'm mad," I grit out, "because we said we'd be careful, but you keep finding stolen moments with me and I'm confused."

"You said we were just friends."

"I'm *trying* to just be friends."

"You're failing."

"You had your *arm around her*—"

"You wore my number," he cuts in, eyes burning. "You sat in the front row, wearing my fucking number. Do you have *any* idea what that did to me? Knowing I coulnd't just come up to you and kiss you."

I freeze.

"You want careful?" he asks. "Because I've been careful. I've been *very* fucking careful. But you look at me like that, and then walk away like you didn't just wreck me in an alleyway five minutes ago, and then *watch me* with someone else like you own me but don't want to claim me, and I'm telling you right now—I'm done playing this halfway bullshit."

My heart's thudding so loud I can barely think.

"I'm not yours," I whisper.

His voice drops lower. Rougher. "Then stop acting like it."

We stare at each other—eyes locked, barely breathing, the air between us thick with everything we're not saying and everything we already know.

I turn and walk away.

Chapter 17

Ethan

She walks away.

Back to the booth. Back to her girls. Back to *wearing my number* like it's a casual choice and not the goddamn reason I can't stop wanting her.

And me?

I'm still standing here, drink in hand, pretending like I'm not two seconds from snapping this glass in half.

She didn't deny it.

Didn't deny the jealousy.

Didn't deny the way she looked at me.

Didn't deny the way her entire body *melted* when I got close.

But she still walked away.

Still said we need to be "careful." Like that means anything when my entire brain has been rewired to respond to one thing and one thing only: *Avery. Maddox.*

I turn back toward the bar.

Liam's there now, nursing a beer like it's judging him.

"You good?" he asks, clearly not expecting a real answer.

I grunt. "Peachy."

He smirks. "Because from here, it looked like you and Connor's sister were about one tequila away from dry-humping in the hallway."

"Shut up."

"Just saying, man. If you're gonna go full rom-com, give us some warning. I'll grab popcorn."

I ignore him, eyes drifting back to the booth. She's laughing at something Rachel said. The sound hits me in the chest harder than any puck I've ever taken to the ribs.

She's smiling.

Acting like she's fine.

Like I'm not still replaying the way her voice broke when she said, *"I'm not yours."*

Not mine.

But she is.

And I think she knows it.

I drain the rest of my drink and set the glass down with more force than necessary. The bartender raises an eyebrow. I wave it off.

Liam's still watching me, eyebrows raised.

"Man, whatever that is," he says, gesturing vaguely toward Avery, "you might want to figure it out. Before it eats you alive."

I don't respond.

He takes another sip of beer, then adds—casually, like it's not a loaded grenade:

"Also? If Connor finds out from *someone else* that you've been sneaking off with his sister? He's gonna fucking kill you."

I freeze.

Because he's right.

Connor's not just a teammate. Not just a goalie. He's *my best friend.* The guy who let me crash in his apartment when my life was burning. The guy who stood by me when the media was chewing me up and spitting me out like yesterday's scandal.

And Avery?

She's his *little sister.*

Off-limits. Untouchable. The one rule I'm not supposed to break.

And I'm breaking it every time I look at her like I already know what she tastes like in the dark.

Liam whistles low. "Just saying, man. Bros before breakdowns."

I don't respond.

Because it's already too late.

Chapter 18

Avery

The Uber ride home is... quiet.

Too quiet.

Connor slides into the front seat like it's just another night out—gives the driver the address, tosses a thanks over his shoulder, and pulls out his phone like he's going to spend the next fifteen minutes updating his fantasy league.

Ethan slides in beside me in the back.

The door shuts.

And suddenly the entire car is filled with... *tension.*

Not the good kind.

Not the kind we *almost* acted on outside.

This is the kind that hums under your skin, sits low in your stomach, and makes it hard to breathe.

We don't speak.

I stare out the window like the night sky's got answers. My hands are clenched in my lap, knuckles white, hoodie sleeves pulled down like I'm trying to shrink into them.

Ethan shifts beside me.

I can feel the heat of his thigh, the solid presence of him. He doesn't move closer. Doesn't touch me.

But he doesn't move away either.

My heartbeat is in my ears.

We hit a red light. The car stops. And in the rearview mirror, I catch it:

Connor's eyes.

Not obvious. Not glaring. Just a glance.

Quick. Sharp.

At Ethan.

Then me.

Then back to his phone.

He doesn't say anything.

Not a joke. Not a question. Not a passive-aggressive chirp about "how cozy the back seat looks."

Just silence.

Which is somehow *so much worse.*

I shift slightly, just enough to give myself an inch more space between me and Ethan, and catch his jaw tightening out of the corner of my eye.

He knows Connor noticed.

I know Connor noticed.

And neither of us is dumb enough to think he's going to let this go.

Just... not tonight.

The rest of the ride is uneventful, except for the part where I actively fight the urge to throw myself out of a moving vehicle to escape the awkwardness.

When we pull up outside the building, Connor hops out first, thanking the driver, already half-distracted by his phone.

Ethan lets me out next.

He doesn't touch me. Doesn't say a word.

Just holds the door open, lets me pass, and follows behind like gravity's doing all the work.

And when we get upstairs?

Connor just says, "Night," and disappears into his room.

No questions.

No confrontation.

Just that *look*.

That quiet, knowing *something* that's going to come back to bite me.

Hard.

I turn to Ethan.

He's watching me.

Like always.

"You think he knows?" I whisper.

His voice is low. "He probably suspects something. Everyone else seems to have clicked on. We don't seem to have a handle on our behavior in public."

"Shit."

He nods. "Yup."

And then we're standing there, alone again, hallway dim, hearts racing.

Still not touching.

Still too close.

Still completely fucked.

Chapter 19

Avery

When Connor texts, *"Dinner at home tonight. Be here,"* I expect takeout and one of his impromptu monologues about team fitness or how Rachel has been haunting his brain like a hot ghost.

What I don't expect is garlic, candles, and a table actually set for three.

"You okay?" I ask, stepping into the apartment and sniffing like a bloodhound. "What's all this?"

Connor grins from the kitchen. "Relax. Just decided to cook. You and Wilson are always coming and going, I hardly see you both. Thought we could hang out for once."

Before I can question that weirdly specific phrasing, the front door opens again.

Ethan.

He freezes for a second when he sees me already here. We make eye contact, and I feel that familiar jolt in my chest. The one that says, *Oh no. We're not normal around each other anymore.*

Connor wipes his hands on a towel. "Perfect. Everyone's here. Sit down before the garlic bread burns."

We both move like suspects in a crime scene—cautious, wary, trying not to make noise. Connor's already pulling plates from the oven like this is a completely normal roommate bonding moment and not low-key psychological warfare.

We sit. I end up next to Ethan. Connor sits across from us like he's about to take notes.

"So," he says, cutting into his pasta. "How do you feel training is going?"

Ethan nods. "Good. Feeling solid. Season started strong."

"And you?" he asks me, like this is all just casual small talk and not a carefully planned interrogation. "You settling in okay?"

"Yeah," I say. "The apartment's great. Thank you for letting me stay."

"Good," Connor says, reaching for the wine bottle. "Nice to have you both here. Feels more balanced."

I don't say anything. Ethan definitely doesn't say anything. We are both very, very busy chewing.

Connor pours us all wine.

"I mean, the place was getting a little too bro-y," he adds with a grin. "Now I come home and the blankets are all folded and we have more than just protein powder in."

Ethan snorts. "You're welcome."

Connor turns to me. "And what's with you wearing his number the other night?"

My spine stiffens.

Ethan shifts beside me.

"Looked cool," Connor adds with a shrug. "Didn't know you were a fan of the Wilson brand."

"It was a... gesture," I say slowly. "Trying to get into the team spirit, trying to get along like you asked."

"Mmhmm." He takes a sip of wine, says nothing else.

And now Ethan's doing that jaw flex thing. Like he's either holding in a guilty secret or trying to telepathically set off the fire alarm so we can flee.

Connor keeps talking—stories from practice, jokes about Carter and Liam, a half-hearted complaint about protein powder all over his gym bag—but I can feel it. The undercurrent. The *not quite said.*

He's watching us.

Not suspicious. Not angry.

Just... watching.

And when Ethan accidentally brushes my hand reaching for the bread basket and we both flinch like we've been tasered?

Connor doesn't blink.

He just sips his wine, like this is exactly the response he expected.

After dinner, we clear plates. Ethan volunteers to do the dishes, which is so out of character I nearly choke. I help dry. Connor leans against the counter with his wine and a smug little half-smile that I swear he *knows* he's wearing.

"Good talk, good food, no bloodshed," he says. "Solid night, we should do it more."

Ethan mumbles something, but I can't hear him and then he wonders off.

I excuse myself to fold laundry I absolutely don't need to fold.

Connor doesn't stop us. He doesn't accuse. He doesn't hint.

But as I walk away, I feel his eyes on both of us. Not unkind. Not disapproving.

Just... *measuring.*

What does this mean?

We don't say a word until the door to the kitchen swings shut behind us.

Ethan walks one step ahead, his hand running through his hair like it's the only thing keeping him from combusting. I trail behind, heart hammering, nerves shot to hell.

Once we hit the hallway—blessed, silent, dimly lit—I grab his arm and pull him to a stop.

"What the actual fuck was that dinner?"

He exhales hard. "A trap. It was a trap, right?"

"I don't know," I hiss. "He was either being normal or *trying to make us sweat.* And the worst part is, I don't know which is scarier."

Ethan leans back against the wall like his spine can't carry the stress anymore. "He brought up the jersey number, Avery. And was cool about it."

"He brought it up like a *casual topic.* No judgment. Just... chilling. Observing. Like some kind of emotional Bond villain."

"I swear to God he was timing how long I looked at you during dinner."

"He gave you equal wine," I say. "Equal. Like he was dividing assets in a divorce."

Ethan groans. "We're fucked."

I cross my arms. "Or he knows and doesn't care."

Ethan looks at me. "Do you believe that?"

"...No. I think he cares a *lot.*"

We stare at each other in that tight, airless silence that's starting to feel familiar. Everything unsaid between us wrapped in tension and smirking big brother energy.

"I didn't even touch you," Ethan mutters. "Not once."

"That's probably what gave it away," I say. "We were acting like we'd just signed an HR agreement not to make eye contact."

He smiles, but it's all stress and exhaustion. "What do we do?"

I step closer. Close enough to smell the aftershave he always uses, the one that drives me crazy. "We act normal."

Ethan lifts a brow. "Define normal."

"Roommates. Friends. Casual hallway chats. Zero suspicious glances. Zero heat."

"Zero heat?" he echoes, clearly offended.

"Not a flicker."

His jaw tightens. "You gonna enforce that rule?"

"I'm trying," I whisper. "But every time you look at me like that—"

"Like what?"

"You look at me like I'm already yours."

His breath catches.

I step back before I do something reckless. Again.

He lets me.

Barely.

Then he mutters, "This is hell."

I nod. "Welcome to roommate bootcamp. You'll be tested on your self-control daily."

Ethan's eyes darken, and for a second—just a second—I think he's going to kiss me right there against the wall.

But he doesn't.

He just leans down, voice rough. "One of us is going to break."

"Yeah," I whisper. "But not tonight."

We part.

Carefully.

And behind the kitchen door, Connor loads a dish into the dishwasher like a man who didn't just play puppet master over an entire emotionally tense meal.

Chapter 20

Ethan

The locker room is loud.

Not unusual. But this morning, it's louder than usual—like someone spiked the Gatorade with caffeine and chaos.

Carter's shirtless, slapping his helmet like it's a drum set. Liam is ranking the team based on who he'd trust to file his taxes. (No one, apparently. Not even himself.)

And Connor?

He's quiet.

Not angry. Not sulking. Just watching. Focused in that calm-before-the-snipe kind of way.

He's been like this all week—less vocal, more observant. Like he's waiting for someone else to make the wrong move so he doesn't have to.

Naturally, Liam sees this as an opportunity to be a menace.

"Hey, Connor," he says, towel over his shoulder. "How's Rachel?"

Connor doesn't even look up. "Alive, I think."

Carter whistles. "Oof. That bad?"

"She's not my girlfriend."

"Could've fooled me," Liam says, grabbing his water bottle. "You were all over her at the bar. Right, Wilson?"

I lift my hands. "I don't comment on other people's disasters."

Connor finally glances up. "Thank you. A man with integrity."

Carter snorts. "Please. This guy had half the bar checking him out after the game and didn't even blink. What's going on with you, anyway?"

I don't answer right away.

Liam jumps in. "Yeah, seriously. Wilson's been suspiciously tame lately. No blurry TikToks. No bar hookups. Not even a walk of shame. What gives, Romeo?"

Before I can redirect or lie—or both—the door swings open.

"Gentlemen," Lexi says, stepping in like she owns the place, camera bag slung over one shoulder. "If I see one more sock on the snack table, I'm setting fire to the protein powder."

Carter straightens up. "Lexi. Wow. You look—professional."

"Save it," she says, already scanning for lighting. "Smile, hydrate, and give me something that reads 'focused athletes' instead of 'adult daycare with sharp objects.'"

Liam grins. "What's the vibe, Lex? Grit? Sweat? Unhinged team brotherhood?"

"I'll take anything that doesn't get me demonetized."

Lexi starts snapping candids. I get tagged for a few shots pulling on gear. She wants something serious—"Game Face Wilson," as she puts it.

Connor walks behind me and grabs one of the protein pancakes off the snack table, talking to Carter just loud enough for me to hear.

"You know, Avery made pancakes better than that last week."

I freeze, only slightly. Don't look. Don't bite.

Carter laughs. "Since when does she cook?"

"She doesn't. But she's learning. She seems... distracted lately, though. Probably all the work stuff."

Then Connor walks off, calm as ever. Whistling.

What's his deal?

Chapter 21

Avery

The team jersey fits better today. - I had to wear his number again - superstitions and all that, we won when I wore it at the last home game.

And I wanted to wear his number. I wanted him to see me in it.

The arena's buzzing already. Home game. Second of the season. The crowd's electric, and the team's energy feels sharp, focused, just this side of cocky. The girls—Lexi, Rachel, Maya, and *finally* Mia, freshly arrived in town and already judging everyone—have claimed our usual seats right behind the bench.

"You went full jersey this time," Maya says, nudging me with a knowing look. "No backwards hat, no denim jacket for camouflage. This is a declaration of war."

"It's just a shirt," I lie.

"Uh-huh," Rachel says, already halfway through a jumbo pretzel. "And I follow Ethan on Instagram for his deep thoughts."

Lexi smirks. "To be fair, he did post a quote last week."

"It was from *Fast & Furious 6*," Maya deadpans.

We're still laughing when the team hits the ice.

Carter's the first to notice us—specifically *me*. He skates by the boards, does a double take, and grins like someone just handed him a rumor wrapped in a bow.

"Hey, Avery!" he calls, voice loud enough to echo off the glass. "When are you gonna wear *my* number?"

The entire bench erupts in hoots and jeers.

Liam yells, "Yeah, let's do a rotation system! Fair's fair!"

Someone else shouts, "We do birthday requests!"

Lexi immediately starts recording. "This is going to be so good."

I'm about to die of secondhand embarrassment when, without warning, Connor barrels past Ethan on the ice—shoulder checking him mid-stride, not enough to knock him over, but enough to make everyone notice.

The energy shifts.

The guys look over.

Like they suddenly remember, *oh right,* she's his sister.

The silence that follows is short-lived but powerful.

Connor doesn't say anything.

He doesn't have to.

The look he gives Carter is pure I-will-end-your-bloodline energy.

The look he gives Ethan?

That's even worse.

Because it's not angry.

It's... a warning.

Ethan doesn't flinch.

But he doesn't smile either.

I fold my arms across my chest, trying not to melt into the concrete.

"Should we be worried?" Mia murmurs beside me. "Because I just watched two grown men have a full emotional breakdown using only eye contact."

Rachel grins. "Nah. That's just what foreplay looks like in sports."

There's something off about the game tonight.

The crowd's roaring, the pace is fast, and Ethan's playing like he's been personally wronged by gravity. He's aggressive, sharp, landing every pass with sniper precision, and skating like the ice owes him money.

But the tension on the ice? It's palpable. You can feel it in the hits. The passes that are a little too hard. The way Connor keeps chirping him—not in the usual friendly banter way. In a *pointed* way.

"You see that?" Lexi says, nudging me hard.

I blink. "What?"

"Connor just yelled 'keep your head in the game, Romeo!' after Ethan missed that rebound."

Rachel perks up. "Okay, that's weirdly specific. Like... Shakespeare-level petty."

Maya frowns. "Did he call him *Romeo* during last game?"

"No," Lexi says slowly, eyes narrowing. "He did not."

Down on the bench, Carter's looking back and forth between them like he's trying to do psychic damage control. Ethan says something under his breath. Connor doesn't even look at him, just shakes his head and mutters something back.

Then they both slam their helmets on and head back out for the next shift.

"You think he knows?" I ask quietly, heart thumping.

Mia doesn't even blink. "Oh, baby girl. He *definitely* knows."

Another hit.

Another pass that comes in just a hair too hot.

And then, mid-play, Connor shoves Ethan after the whistle and says something we can't hear—but whatever it is, it makes Ethan *snap his head around* and glare like he's five seconds from dropping gloves.

"Jesus," Lexi mutters. "Okay, I'm calling it. This isn't hockey tension. This is I-know-you-made-out-with-my-sister-in-my-bathroom tension."

Rachel whistles. "Ten bucks says he brings it up mid-period."

"I should go down there," I say, half-standing.

"Absolutely not," Lexi says, yanking me back. "Do you want to make it worse?"

"I *might* want to make it worse," I hiss.

Maya holds up her phone, camera already rolling. "Well if you do, I've got the popcorn angle ready."

Connor makes another save.

Ethan scores off the next faceoff like his life depends on it.

But when they skate past each other, there's no celebration.

No high five.

Just tension.

Simmering, undeniable, team-imploding tension.

And I realize—with a pit in my stomach—that if we're not careful, this whole thing?

It's going to blow up.

The team wins.

Barely.

Ethan scores twice. Connor makes a glove save so ridiculous even the opposing fans applaud. And when the final buzzer sounds, it's pure adrenaline and roaring crowds and sweaty group hugs that smell like victory and regret.

The tension doesn't break—it *shifts.*

It follows us to the house party.

Some rando's place in the hills, already packed with players, friends, and the occasional influencer trying to tag the team's location for clout. Someone's DJing out of a laundry room. There's glitter in the air, I swear to God. And Carter's already shirtless in the backyard threatening to backflip off the hot tub.

Ethan's somewhere inside.

Connor's beside me.

And I feel like I'm standing in the eye of a hurricane where everyone else is partying but the pressure hasn't dropped yet.

"You want a drink?" Connor asks, handing me a Solo cup like this is *any* normal night.

I blink. "Uh. Sure?"

He clinks his against mine. "You look good, by the way."

Okay. Weird.

"Thanks?" I say cautiously.

"You wore the jersey again," he adds, sipping casually. "Thought it was just a one-time thing."

My heart stutters. I force a smile. "Guess I'm more superstitious than I thought."

He nods, not even looking at me.

Then he says, "You and I—we're good. Always."

What the hell does that mean?

I glance around. "Where's Ethan?"

He shrugs. "Floating. Probably avoiding me."

"So... nothing's wrong?"

He turns to me with the calmest, most unnerving smile I've ever seen. "Why would something be wrong?"

"I don't know. Maybe because you've spent the entire week passive-aggressively body-checking your best friend."

Connor chuckles like I've just accused him of *light jaywalking.* "He's fine."

"You sure?"

"Yeah." He drains his drink. "It's Ethan. He can take a hit."

That's when I spot Ethan across the room—leaning against the kitchen island, beer in hand, watching us like he's calculating whether he's about to get murdered in a very polite way.

His jaw is tight.

His eyes flick from me to Connor and back like he's waiting for a punchline that never comes.

"Maybe you should talk to him," I say, gentle.

Connor shrugs. "Theres nothing to talk about, we are good."

And just like that—he walks off. Smiling. Laughing with Carter. Acting like *nothing happened.*

Leaving me standing there with a cup of mystery liquid and a deep, unshakeable feeling that this entire night is a setup for something none of us are ready for.

Chapter 22

Ethan

I last thirteen minutes inside the house party before I need air.

Too loud. Too hot. Too many people talking about the win like I didn't spend half the game getting chirped by my best friend while trying not to look at his sister like I want to ruin her on every surface in his apartment.

I duck out the back, past the beer pong table and Carter's off-brand DJ set, past girls in heels and guys yelling about post-game stats like any of it matters.

And then I'm behind the pool house. Alone.

Or I think I am—until I hear footsteps.

Her footsteps.

I turn just as Avery steps into the dim light, wearing *my* number and looking like sin bottled in soft curves and wildfire eyes.

"Hey," she says, voice soft but steady.

I swear it almost undoes me.

"Hey."

She walks toward me slowly, like she's approaching a live wire. Like she knows touching me means getting burned. "You okay?"

I shake my head. "Not even close."

She exhales, stepping in beside me, arms crossed. "Connor's being... different."

"He's being a mindfuck," I mutter. "I don't know if he wants to throw me off my game or throw me through a wall."

"He was nice to me," she says, like it's a confession. "Really nice. Like... suspiciously nice."

"He knows."

She blinks. "You sure?"

"Yeah." I look at her—really look at her. "He's playing with me. Every time I think he's gonna crack, he just smiles. It's *unnerving*."

She chews her lip. "You think I made it worse by wearing the jersey again?"

"No." I step closer. "You made it worse the second you walked into my life."

"Thanks," she says dryly.

I grin. "And by worse I mean *better in every way and also completely fucking unmanageable*."

Her laugh is soft. And holy shit, it wrecks me.

I close the space between us.

"You know this is a bad idea," she whispers.

"Disaster," I agree. "But I'm doing it anyway."

And then I crash my mouth into hers.

It's not soft. It's not careful. It's two weeks of tension and a season's worth of frustration exploding between us. She gasps against me, and I take that opportunity to slide my hands down her back, gripping tight and hauling her up.

She wraps her legs around my waist like she was *waiting* for this—like she *knew*.

I press her up against the nearest tree, bark rough against her spine, my hands on her thighs, her fingers buried in my hair.

"You drive me insane," I murmur against her mouth.

"I know," she breathes, kissing me harder.

I grind into her, just enough to feel her whimper, just enough to make my self-control fracture like glass.

"You have any idea what you do to me?" I growl.

She smirks, lips brushing mine. "Judging by the part of you currently trying to start a forest fire through your jeans... yeah. I've got a clue."

I groan, biting gently at her lower lip. "We can't keep doing this."

"Then put me down."

I don't move.

She grins. "That's what I thought."

I reach for my back pocket—out of habit, out of some last shred of sanity—and she stops me with a hand on my chest.

"You don't need it," she says, voice breathless but clear.

I blink. "What?"

"I have an IUD," she murmurs, eyes locked on mine. "And I'm clean."

Fuck.

That word hits different when she says it. Sharp. Honest. No games.

I exhale, my forehead dropping to hers. "You sure?"

"Yes."

I run my hand down her thigh, try to breathe through the storm building behind my ribs. "I'm clean too. I haven't been with anyone since I was last tested, about a month before you came."

Her eyes flicker. "You haven't—?"

"No, no one," I say, voice rough.

That does something to her. I feel it in the way her breath catches. The way her hips shift against mine like she needs me *now.*

I press her back to the tree again and line myself up—skin to skin, no barrier, nothing between us but months of tension and the kind of hunger that burns through morals.

She gasps when I push in—slow, deep, real.

Every fucking inch.

We both groan at the same time—like the relief is too much. Like it's been building and building and now we're finally allowed to let go.

"Oh my God," she whispers, voice already shaking.

"You feel—" I choke on the words. "Jesus, Avery. You're perfect."

She clutches my shoulders like she's holding on for dear life. "Move."

And I do.

Hard. Deep. No space left between us.

The feel of her—hot and tight and *real*—nearly makes me lose control. Every time I thrust, she gasps. Every time I grind in deeper, she moans my name like it's a promise and a curse.

We're both sweating. Panting. Lost.

The tree scrapes at her back, my hands bruise her hips, and still—she wants more.

"Ethan," she breathes. "Don't stop. Don't you *dare* stop."

"Not a chance."

I fuck into her like I'm making a point. Like I want to rewrite every memory of every guy who ever made her feel small. Every bastard who doubted her. Every name that tried to drag hers through the mud.

She's mine.

Right now, in this moment—she's fucking mine.

Her thighs tighten. Her breath goes shallow. And I know she's close.

"Let go," I whisper against her throat. "Come on me. Just like this. Let me feel it."

She does—with a strangled cry, body clenching around me so hard I nearly black out.

I lose it right after—groaning against her skin, spilling into her with a low, broken sound that tears out of my chest like a prayer I didn't know I had in me.

We stay tangled, bodies still pressed together, sweat and heat and breathless silence hanging in the air.

Her head rests on my shoulder.

My hand strokes her back, slow.

She lifts her head after a minute, eyes dazed, lips swollen.

"That was—"

"Yeah," I say. "It fucking was."

Chapter 23

Avery

I walk back into the party first.

Alone.

Hair finger-combed, skin still warm, legs barely functioning like a normal person. I know I should feel embarrassed—or at the very least, *concerned*—that I just had the best sex of my life against a goddamn tree while my brother is thirty feet away doing keg stands with a girl named Tasha.

But all I feel is light.

Floaty.

Feral-forest-nymph-just-claimed-a-hockey-player kind of light.

I slip into the kitchen, pretending to be extremely interested in the snacks. Lexi spots me immediately.

She narrows her eyes. "You disappeared."

"Bathroom," I lie, very badly.

Maya looks up from her drink. "For thirty minutes?"

"Long line." I grab a chip like it's going to save me. "Girls' line."

Lexi gives me one of those *bitch, I invented that excuse* looks and sips her drink with dangerous calm.

Then she leans in. "You're glowing."

"Am not."

"Please. You have the exact energy of someone who just got railed and loved it."

Maya spits her drink.

Lexi doesn't even blink. "Tell me I'm wrong."

I open my mouth—and that's when Ethan walks in.

Five minutes later. Solo. Slightly flushed. Shirt rumpled. Hair a mess. Probably still smelling as much like sex as I do.

Lexi's eyebrows *launch into orbit.*

"Oh my God," she whispers. "You're not even trying to hide it."

"I am trying," I hiss.

"You're *failing.*"

Maya, deadpan: "So are we using code names for this situation or just calling it what it is. I have never seen him so invested in someone, sorry Lexi."

"Oh I am so happy he's finally found someone that brings out the best in him, I just hope Connor see's how happy you both are. I have never seen Ethan like this and I have known him for quite a few years." Lexi says as she sips her drink.

"Stop," I mutter. "He's coming over—stop!"

And just as I'm preparing to die, Connor steps between us.

"Hey," he says, cool as anything, holding a drink.

Ethan freezes.

Connor claps a hand on his shoulder. "You good, man?"

"Yeah," Ethan says too fast.

"Cool, cool." Connor takes a sip. "You've got a little something on your neck."

Ethan blinks. "What?"

Connor smirks. "Looks like tree bark or mud?"

Lexi chokes on her drink. I consider climbing into the fridge and never returning.

"Oh," Connor adds casually, "Avery—your lip gloss is smeared, are you alright?"

I touch my mouth instinctively.

He smiles wider.

"I'll go round up the boys, maybe we should all do some shots?" he says, and walks off like he didn't just nuke our entire ability to pretend.

Ethan exhales.

Lexi stares at me. "He knows."

Maya nods solemnly. "He 100% knows."

I drain my drink.

And whisper to myself, "We are so fucking screwed."

The bar is loud.

Shoulder-to-shoulder hockey players, drinks clinking, music vibrating through the floorboards. It's post-game chaos with a side of beer and bravado, and somehow I've found myself squeezed between Lexi and Maya in a booth that smells like citrus vodka and secrets.

Ethan's across the bar. Laughing. Tension in his shoulders. That smile that only shows up when he forgets to be haunted. It makes my chest ache—in the good way.

Connor returns with a full tray of shots like some unhinged bartender-slash-hostage negotiator.

"Alright," he yells over the music. "Let's raise a glass."

Everyone grabs one. Tequila. Of course.

I reach for mine, but Lexi stops me with a light touch on my arm. "Wait. He's about to speech."

Connor stands tall at the edge of the table, the unofficial king of this little post-game kingdom. Everyone goes quiet—well, *quieter*—because when Connor raises his glass, you shut up and listen.

"To family," he starts. "To wins. To the first game of the season being a hell of a way to kick things off."

Cheers.

"To the best team in the league," he continues. "And to new faces..."

His eyes flick to me.

I smile politely. Why do I feel like a deer in a very charming, *extremely smug* set of headlights?

"...I just want to say thanks to everyone for welcoming my sister."

Lexi mutters "uh-oh" under her breath. Maya just sips her drink and watches like it's a Netflix special.

Connor keeps going, smiling like this is all very casual.

"And also, huge thanks to my boys for keeping their distance—appreciate the respect."

The table chuckles. A few whoops. Liam shouts "Can't promise I'll behave forever!" which earns him a death glare and a foot stomp under the table from Lexi.

Connor's smile doesn't slip.

"Seriously," he adds, tone still light, "she's my blood. You all know I wouldn't cope well if anyone—*anyone*—laid a hand on her."

He raises his glass higher.

"So let's drink to family. And to *not* sending me to prison for murder."

Everyone laughs.

Except Ethan.

He chokes on his shot like he forgot how to swallow.

I stare at Connor. He clinks glasses with Liam, then Carter, and finally, me.

He winks. "Glad you're here, Aves."

I force a smile. "Glad to be here."

My drink tastes like tequila and *tension.*

Lexi leans in. "That was so subtle, I almost applauded."

Maya nods. "He's basically threatening everyone with a smile. Impressive."

Across the bar, Ethan coughs again. Carter's patting his back while whispering something that makes his ears go red.

And Connor?

Connor's grinning.

Because *he knows.*

And he's going to make sure every second of this night feels like a countdown to Ethan's slow emotional execution.

I find Connor near the bar, laughing too loud at something Carter said and half-watching Ethan out of the corner of his eye like he's tracking prey, not drinking with friends.

I touch his arm.

"Hey," I say, voice low. "Can we take a walk?"

He glances down at me, all easy smiles and mischief. "You planning to lecture me about the toast? Because that was gold."

"No," I murmur. "Just a walk."

Something in my tone must land, because he sobers slightly and nods.

We step outside into the cool night air. The street's quieter than the party, still humming from bass and bodies, but out here, it's just the two of us. Siblings. A goalie and the girl he's always tried to keep safe.

I cross my arms, unsure where to start. Connor kicks a stone across the pavement like we're twelve again and I just told him someone called me a name on the school bus.

"You alright?" he asks.

"Yeah. I just..." I swallow. "Wanted to ask you something."

"Okay."

I take a breath. "Why don't you want me dating anyone on your team?"

He pauses. The silence stretches. Then he gives a soft chuckle and looks down at the ground.

"Because I know them," he says.

"Connor—"

"I *love* them," he cuts in, voice steady. "They're my brothers. My ride-or-die idiots. I'd take a punch for any one of them."

A pause.

"But they're not good enough for you."

I blink. "You don't think I can choose someone who is good enough for me?"

He looks at me then—really looks. And I see it, plain as day: the worry. The big-brother fear. The lingering guilt that maybe he didn't protect me enough before.

"You've been through hell, Aves," he says, softer now. "And you survived it. You don't need more chaos. You need peace. Someone who puts you first. Someone who'd fight for you, and fight to be with you."

"I'm not breakable," I whisper.

"I *know* that. Doesn't mean I don't want better for you."

His voice is rough now. Strained. The way it gets when he's trying too hard to stay chill while the inside of him's unraveling.

He leans against the railing, staring out at the street. "Do you know how many times I've watched those guys bring someone home and forget her name by morning? Or get drunk and disappear into corners with puck bunnies like it's a sport off the ice too?"

He glances at me, eyes fierce.

"I couldn't live with myself if one of them did that to *you.*"

My throat tightens. My hands shake just a little.

"I'm not asking for your permission," I say quietly.

He nods. "I know. But I'm still your brother. And I still want to protect you—even if you don't want it."

I look away. The words bubble up like champagne behind my ribs, sharp and fizzy and dangerous.

I want to tell him.

I *almost* tell him.

That it's Ethan. That it's not just sex or a bad decision or a game. That it *matters.*

That he makes me feel safe in a way no one has in years.

But the words stay stuck behind my teeth.

Because I don't want to break this moment. Not when Connor's being raw and real. Not when he's showing me how much he still sees me as that girl he used to carry piggyback down the driveway after a bad fall.

So instead, I just nod.

And lie.

"I get it."

He puts an arm around me. "I know I'm intense. But it's only because I love you, Aves."

"I know."

We stand there a little longer. The quiet between us isn't heavy—just full. Full of things unsaid, feelings unspoken, truths we're not ready to drop yet.

Not tonight.

The door swings open.

Laughter pours out—the warm, beer-soaked kind. Music thrumming underfoot. The smell of alcohol and confidence and too many colognes mixing in the air.

I step inside.

And freeze.

They're standing near the bar.

Ethan. Liam. And three puck bunnies—*the* puck bunnies. Perfect hair, glossy lips, tits defying gravity and logic. One of them leans in close to Ethan, her fingers brushing his arm like she owns him. Like she's already planning where she's going to leave her lipstick.

He's smiling. Laughing at something Liam says. Another girl tilts her head, giggling, hand on his chest.

I don't even breathe.

My feet won't move. My throat tightens. My stomach lurches in a way that feels unfairly familiar—too close to the way it did when I watched someone else do this to me. *Be mine behind closed doors, but everyone else's when the lights come up.*

He didn't see me.

He doesn't know I'm here.

And I didn't stay long enough to see what he'd do.

A hand lands on my arm—light, but firm.

Connor.

He followed me back in, quieter than I thought he would be. His eyes flick between me and the scene at the bar. Then he sighs—deep, long, disappointed.

And when he speaks, his voice is low. Steady. Too steady.

"This is exactly what I meant."

I swallow. "Connor—"

"They're all like this," he says. "They don't mean to be. It's just what the job makes them. They thrive on attention. The game's part of it—but so are the girls. The noise. The chaos."

I clench my jaw. My heart's doing this stupid stuttering thing in my chest. I feel stupid. Embarrassed. *Small.*

"You deserve more than someone who forgets what he has when someone shinier walks up," Connor adds.

I say nothing.

Because part of me wants to scream *you didn't see what I saw.*

And another part whispers *he's not like them.*

But the loudest voice?

The one that says *maybe you were wrong.*

I turn to Connor, voice thin. "Can we go home, please?"

He nods once. Doesn't push. Just puts a hand on the small of my back and walks me out, like I'm breakable glass he suddenly remembers he's holding.

And I don't look back.

Because I already know what I'd see.

Chapter 24

Ethan

The bar is too loud.

Liam's shouting about something, gesturing with a beer in one hand and a mozzarella stick in the other like he's conducting an orchestra of cholesterol.

I laugh half-heartedly, still riding the high from the win, but something's off. I can't shake it.

And then they show up.

Three of them. Tall. Legs for days. Lips like weapons. Standard post-game puck bunny formation. One of them is already reaching for my arm like we've done this before. Like she knows I'll be interested.

I step back, casually. "Hey."

"Hey yourself," one purrs, all teeth and perfume. "Big win tonight, number 21."

Her friend giggles. "You played so good. So aggressive."

"Thanks," I say, polite but distant. My voice doesn't match the expression they're used to seeing. I keep my arms down. Shoulders back. No invitation.

The third one leans in. "You celebrating after this?"

Liam, the unhelpful bastard, grins. "Always. That's the Wilson way."

I glare at him. He shrugs and downs the rest of his drink like innocence was never an option.

"Look," I say, trying to keep it friendly but firm, "I appreciate it, really. But I'm not—"

"Oh, come on," one interrupts. "Don't tell me you've got a girlfriend."

"No," I answer. Too fast. Too honest. "Just... not in the market."

They pout like I've just canceled Christmas.

"You sure?" the boldest one asks, running a finger lightly up my forearm. "We're really fun."

Before I can respond, Liam jumps in like he's a damn guardian angel with a mullet. "Hey, sorry to cut this off, ladies, but my guy here's gotta check in with the coach. Big media stuff tomorrow. You get it."

"Wait—" one starts, but Liam grabs my elbow and pulls.

I don't resist.

"Coach?" I mutter as we cut across the bar.

"Shut up, I panicked," he says. "You looked like a hostage. I wasn't letting you get seduced into a public scandal."

I snort. "Thanks."

He claps me on the back. "You owe me mozzarella."

But even as we laugh, my eyes scan the crowd. No sign of Avery. Or Connor. Or literally *anyone* I want to talk to.

I check my phone.

Nothing.

I frown and head outside. The air hits cold and sharp against my skin.

I text Connor.

Me:

You guys bail already?

It takes two minutes before I get a reply.

Connor:
Avery wasn't feeling well. Took her home.
That's it. No smiley face. No banter. Just facts.
I stare at the message like it's a puzzle I don't have all the pieces for.
Wasn't feeling well?
Did something happen?
Why didn't she wait?
I stare out at the street, hoping for an answer that doesn't come.

I'm still standing on the curb when the door swings open behind me.
Liam steps out, still riding the post-win buzz, a half-empty beer in one hand and concern buried underneath all the usual smartassery.
"Yo," he says, walking up beside me. "You good?"
"Yeah," I lie.
After a beat, he shrugs. "I live, like, ten minutes from here. Wanna crash at mine?"
I glance at him. "Seriously?"
"Yeah. I got pizza rolls in the freezer and a couch that's only slightly concave from emotional damage."
I hesitate.
Avery's gone. Connor's gone. I don't want to go back to that apartment and wonder what she's thinking. I definitely don't want to lay in that bed and scroll through texts I'm not brave enough to send.
"Yeah," I say. "Yeah, sure. May as well."
Liam nods, casual. "Cool. You can borrow my old team shirt to sleep in. It says *Slapshots and Bad Decisions*. Felt fitting."

"Story of my life," I mutter.

He smirks. "C'mon, heartbreak. Let's go eat carbs and pretend your life isn't imploding."

I follow him to his car.

Because honestly?

Right now, pretending sounds like the only thing I'm good at.

Chapter 25

Avery

The sun's too bright when I wake up.

Too cheerful for someone who feels like her chest's been hollowed out and filled with fire.

I sit up slowly, tug my hoodie down over my thighs, and shuffle out of the guest room.

The apartment is silent.

I pass the bathroom. Empty.

Then... Ethan's door.

Open.

Bed still made. Pillows untouched. The same team sweatshirt folded neatly at the foot of the mattress like he never came back at all.

My stomach drops.

He didn't come home.

He *didn't come home.*

The ache hits so fast I don't even have time to brace for it. Just a sudden, crushing pressure in my chest like my ribs are collapsing in on themselves.

Of course.

Of *course* he didn't.

Those girls were practically on his lap. Laughing, touching, offering everything. And me? I left with my brother like a coward, sick to my stomach over something I couldn't even say out loud.

And Ethan?

He probably didn't even notice I was gone.

I close his door slowly and walk back into the kitchen like I'm on autopilot. I don't need breakfast. I need answers.

But all I have is a phone.

So I grab it.

Thumbs flying, fingers shaking.

Group Chat: 🐎🌿❗Chaos Coven

Avery:

I'm so fucking stupid.

Three dots appear instantly.

Lexi:

Oh shit, what happened?

Maya:

Girl. We're ready. Who do we fight.

Avery:

He didn't come home. His bed hasn't been touched. I saw him with those girls and I knew it. I knew I was just a game.

Lexi:

Wait—are you sure? Like maybe he—

Avery:

He was laughing. Letting them touch him. I left and he didn't even follow. Didn't text. Didn't check. Nothing.

Maya:

Do you want us to key his car or do you want tea first?

Avery:

Honestly? Both.

I drop the phone on the counter and grip the edge of it hard.

Because this isn't about one night. It's not even about sex.

It's about me *letting* someone in again.

About *believing* someone when they said I was different.

And now?

Now I feel like an idiot.

30 minutes later theres a knock at the door—its sounds like code for *we're outside, open up before we key someone's car out of emotional solidarity.*

I crack the door and instantly get mobbed.

Lexi breezes in first, holding coffee like a peace treaty and smelling like expensive war. "Okay. We brought caffeine, croissants, and emotional backup. Who are we killing?"

Maya follows behind her with a canvas bag of snacks and something that looks suspiciously like a bottle of wine. "We're here to stage a very supportive, very subtle intervention."

Rachel struts in last, tossing her hair like she's walking a runway. "And I just missed you. Obviously."

I blink at them. "How did you—?"

"Group chat panic texts are sacred," Lexi says, setting the drinks down. "You basically summoned us."

"And we're dropping by totally casually," Maya adds, not casually at all.

"We figured you might want company," Rachel says, giving me a look that says *we know you're spiraling, but we brought backup and bread.*

I try to smile. I really do. But the ache from this morning is still raw, and seeing Ethan's untouched bed keeps looping through my head like a breakup montage with no actual relationship to mourn.

And then—Connor appears.

Barefoot, hoodie on, hair messy like he just woke up from the dead. He stops dead when he sees the three girls in his kitchen.

"Um. Morning?" he says slowly.

Lexi turns on her best *polite stranger* voice. "Connor. Hi. We were just in the area. Thought we'd bring Avery coffee. Girls' morning."

Maya nods like she rehearsed it. "Totally impromptu."

Rachel? She says nothing. Just sips her latte and looks *entirely too calm.*

Connor eyes her. "Rachel."

"Connor." Her tone is sweet. Innocent. Which means it's absolutely dangerous.

His eyes narrow, like he's trying to figure out *why she's here...* in his kitchen... with a pastry.

Lexi jumps in. "Avery had a rough night. We wanted to cheer her up."

That seems to snap his attention back to me. His face softens.

"You okay?" he asks, voice lower now.

"Fine," I lie.

He nods slowly. "Alright. Just—yell if you need anything. I'll be in my room."

And with one last glance at Rachel (who waves at him with a buttery croissant), he retreats.

The door shuts.

Instant chaos.

Lexi spins on me. "Okay. What the hell happened last night? And why was Ethan not in his bed?"

Maya plops down on the couch. "Also, when did things get intense between Rachel and Connor?"

Rachel raises her hands. "I don't know what you're talking about."

"They are literally getting worse every time they see each other," Lexi mutters.

Rachel throws a croissant at her.

Meanwhile, I collapse into the armchair and press the coffee to my face like it might absorb the heartbreak through osmosis.

"I think he went home with them," I say quietly.

All three freeze.

Lexi's eyes go deadly sharp. "You *think*?"

"His bed was untouched. He never came back."

Maya hisses. "Okay, but were the puck bunnies *clinging* or just *hovering*?"

"Clinging," I say, voice cracking. "Like *octopus in heels* level."

The room goes quiet for a beat.

Then Lexi says, "Okay. So when do we burn his jersey?"

I'm still hugging my coffee like it might file a restraining order when Lexi moves closer and pulls me into a real hug—tight, no hesitation, like she knows exactly how this kind of heartbreak works.

Because she does.

She pulls back just enough to look at me and says softly, "He's a good guy, Avery. But he does really stupid shit."

I blink, lips parting. "You don't have to say that just because he's your—"

"I'm not saying it for *him*." Her voice is gentle, but unwavering. "I'm saying it because I've been where you are. And I know how much it fucking hurts to care about someone who hasn't figured out how to care about themselves yet."

My throat tightens.

Lexi exhales. "Ethan... he's complicated. I was with him for nearly two years, Avery. We were a mess. We broke each other in ways I'm still not proud of."

I stare at her. "But you're okay now?"

She smiles—small, sad, but real. "Yeah. Because we learned. And because we forgave each other. Eventually."

Rachel, from her perch on the counter, throws in dryly: "And then she went and *married his dad*, because Lexi's not dramatic at all."

Lexi whips a napkin at her face. "I *fell in love* with his dad, thank you very much."

Maya cackles into her coffee. "You realize how insane that sounds, right?"

Rachel smirks. "It's giving Shakespeare, but with more hockey and hotter suits."

Lexi turns back to me, brushing a tear off my cheek with her thumb.

"I know Ethan," she says. "And I know he's probably out there beating himself up over something he didn't even mean to do wrong. He shuts down when he doesn't know how to fix things. But that doesn't mean he doesn't care."

My voice is barely a whisper. "Then why didn't he come home?"

Lexi looks at me for a long moment. Then quietly says, "Maybe he thought you didn't want him to."

My heart stutters. The ache spikes again, new and sharp and laced with doubt.

"I don't know if I can do this," I admit.

"You don't have to," she says. "But if you *want* to? We've got your back. Every step of the way."

Rachel raises her coffee. "To mildly toxic emotional growth."

Maya adds, "And loving idiots with excellent abs."

We all clink cups.

And I laugh—because it's that or cry again. And for now?

Laughing feels like healing.

Two glasses of wine in and I'm emotionally softened like a croissant left in the sun.

Lexi has fully taken over my couch, Rachel's on the rug with her second mimosa (don't ask how that happened), and Maya is leaned back in the armchair like a Bond villain made of empathy and well-timed eyebrow raises.

There's laughter, warmth, carbs everywhere. The soft glow of safe space.

And maybe it's the wine, or the way Lexi looked at me earlier like she *sees* me, but the words slip out before I can stop them.

"So... I got offered a job."

Every head turns.

I swirl the wine in my glass, heart hammering. "Full-time trainer. In Louisiana. It's not exactly the Olympic pipeline, but it's good. Stable. Paid. Dan says it's a clean slate."

Lexi perks up. "That's amazing."

Maya nods. "That's huge, Ave. Like... dream job territory."

I shrug, mouth dry. "They want me out there by next month. But... I've been thinking I might go early. Just... get out. I already agreed to take the job, it would be crazy to turn it down."

Rachel frowns. "Why early?"

I look down at my lap. "Because now... I don't really have a reason to stay. I came to mend, to have me time. But with all this drama with Ethan I feel worse being here."

The silence is sharp, but it doesn't cut me. Not here. Not with them.

Lexi shifts closer. "Avery, that decision has to be yours. Not because of a guy. Not because of drama."

"And definitely not because of one bad night," Maya adds.

Rachel raises her glass. "Even if you do leave, it won't be running away. It'll be choosing yourself. Which, frankly, is hot girl behavior."

I smile, small and sad. "I wasn't sure I wanted it. But now? After everything..."

Lexi takes my hand. "Then do it. We'll support whatever you choose. Even if you run off to ride horses and avoid emotionally repressed hockey players forever."

I open my mouth to say thank you—

When a voice cuts through the moment like a knife.

"You're leaving?"

I freeze.

All of us turn toward the hallway, where Connor stands—hair messy, hoodie sleeves pushed up, eyes locked on me like I just punched him in the throat.

"You're leaving?" he says again, voice tighter now. Hurt. Surprised.

I blink, wine glass suddenly heavy in my hand. "I was just telling the girls—"

"Louisiana?" he interrupts. "That's what this is?"

"I didn't make a decision yet."

"But you're thinking about it," he says, his jaw tight. "Like, seriously thinking about it."

"Connor—" Lexi starts, but he lifts a hand.

His gaze doesn't leave me.

"You weren't even gonna tell me?"

The guilt hits hard and sharp. "I was going to. I just—wanted to be sure before I said anything."

He nods once. Too fast. "Cool. Yeah. No, that's cool."

Then he turns and walks back toward his room.

The girls are dead silent.

Rachel mutters, "Well, that escalated."

Lexi looks at me. "You okay?"

I stare at the empty hallway.

And whisper, "Not really."

It's late.

The kind of quiet where the air feels heavy, like it knows something's about to break.

The girls have gone. The laughter's long since faded. And all I can hear now is the echo of my own thoughts.

I knock gently on Connor's door.

He doesn't answer right away, but after a second: "Yeah?"

I step inside. He's sitting on the edge of the bed, hoodie sleeves pushed up, eyes bloodshot from thinking too hard. He looks at me like he's already bracing for impact.

"Can we talk?" I ask.

He nods. "Sure."

I sit beside him, heart pounding hard enough to bruise my ribs.

"There's something I need to say," I start. "And I need you to let me finish. Please."

His brows furrow, but he nods again. Silent.

"It's about Ethan."

That's when his entire body tenses. His spine goes straight. His jaw locks.

"We didn't mean for it to happen. And I didn't want to lie to you. But... something's been going on. For weeks now." My voice catches, and I push through. "It started the night of the wedding. And it's been complicated and stupid and messy, and I know he's your best friend, but—"

I pause, trying to find the right words. Not too much. Not too little.

"I cared. Still do."

That's all I say. That's all I *can* say.

"I thought maybe it meant something," I whisper. "But I saw him last night, with those girls, and I just... I don't want to be the one who waits around for someone who doesn't choose me."

Connor's staring at the floor like he wants to punch it. His hands are balled into fists. But he doesn't interrupt.

"I talked to Dan earlier. I'm taking the job. He booked me a hotel tonight near the airport. I leave in the morning."

He jerks his head toward me, stunned. "Tomorrow?"

I nod. "It's time to focus on myself, and I think this will be the best thing for me."

His voice is low, rough. "So that's it? You're just... going?"

"I need to," I say. "This was never permanent. It was a reset. A pause. I just didn't expect to have all this happen with Ethan."

He stands up suddenly, pacing. Like he's trying to shake the words out of his system.

"You want me to kick him out?" he asks. "Because I will. You want to stay? I'll throw his ass out tonight."

My heart cracks.

"No," I say softly. "Don't do that."

"Aves—"

"No. That's not what this is about. This isn't about punishing anyone. I don't need that." I look at him, really look. "And you'd hate yourself if you did."

He scrubs a hand over his face. "I just don't get it. Why didn't you tell me?"

"I was trying to protect you. And him. And maybe even myself. But I guess I just made it worse."

Connor sinks back onto the bed like the weight of it all finally knocked him down.

"I hate this," he mutters.

"I know."

"You deserve better than that. Than this."

I sit beside him again. "I'll be okay."

He turns his head toward me. "You're really leaving."

I nod. "Yeah."

A long silence stretches between us. Heavy. Final.

Then, in a whisper:

"Don't tell him. Please."

Connor closes his eyes. "I knew something was going on, you two went from hating each other to being so weird around each other. I just can't believe neither of you had the guts to tell me."

"I don't think we really knew what it was, and maybe it wasn't anything to him. But it meant something to me. That's probably why it hurts so much. But I am not leaving because of him, I am leaving to focus on myself, like I should have done originally."

"You will always have a room here Aves, I love having you here. And I'm so proud of you."

"I love you big bro!"

"Love you too Aves."

We sit there, shoulder to shoulder, not saying anything else.

Because there's nothing left to say.

When I finally stand and walk out, suitcase waiting by my door, I already feel the goodbye hollowing me out.

And I know—

When that flight takes off in the morning, I'm leaving more than just this apartment behind.

Chapter 26

Ethan

I wake up to the blinding sunlight coming through Liam's stupidly expensive loft windows and the sound of him singing *badly* in the shower.

My head's pounding, my mouth's dry, and my body feels like I got hit by a Zamboni wearing heels.

I groan. "Kill me."

From the bathroom:

"Can't! You owe me pancakes for dragging your mopey ass out of that bar before you face-planted into a booth."

Right. Last night. Puck bunnies. Avery leaving early. Connor looking like he wanted to murder someone.

Everything feels... off. But I chalk it up to the hangover.

"Think I might just hang here today," I mutter, grabbing a throw blanket and collapsing back onto the couch. "Might as well milk your hospitality."

Liam shrugs, towel slung around his waist. "Mi casa es bro casa."

We order breakfast, play some FIFA, argue about cereal rankings, and for a few blissful hours, I forget I have a rapidly disintegrating situation waiting back at Connor's.

I finally head home after nine, fully intending to chill for the rest of the night.

The apartment is dark when I step inside. Lights off. Quiet. Eerily quiet.

Connor's room is closed, no surprise. Avery's door... shut too.

A flicker of something weird hits my chest, but I ignore it.

Probably tired. Probably crashed early.

I grab a water from the fridge, chug half of it, then toss my hoodie over the back of a chair and head straight for bed.

No texts. No drama. Just sleep.

I wake up to the sound of my alarm, groaning as I stretch and glance at the time.

8:13 AM.

Shit. Late.

I rush through a shower, throw on my training gear, and step out into the hallway.

Connor's gone. His gear isn't by the door. Coffee mug's missing. So he's already at the rink.

Typical overachiever.

I glance toward Avery's door. Still shut.

She must've slept in.

Or maybe she's just avoiding me after last night.

I frown. I'm not even sure what I did, or if it was even me that upset her. I will catch her later and make sure she's good.

I grab my bag and keys, shoot off a quick *On my way* text to the group chat, and head to the car.

Training awaits.

The second my skates hit the ice, I know something's off.

The energy's weird. Quiet. Like the whole team's holding its breath.

Carter's mid-laugh when he sees me, then immediately clams up. Liam glances at Mason and mutters something I don't catch.

Everyone's eyes shift—away, back, and then zeroed in on me like I've got a target painted on my back.

I frown.

"What the hell is going on?"

Then I see Connor.

Skating toward me like a fucking missile. No stick. No words.

Just fury written all over his face.

"Yo, Connor—" I don't even get to finish.

Crack.

His fist hits my jaw so hard I hear a pop.

Pain explodes across my face. I stagger, boots scraping ice, barely staying upright. "Jesus—what the fuck?!" Before I can breathe, he hits me again.

Hard. Right across the mouth.

"This is for touching my sister!" Connor yells, voice echoing through the rink like a gunshot.

Time slows.

What? "What are you talking ab—" Another punch.

This time to the stomach. I double over, windless, eyes blurring.

"And this is for lying about it," he spits. "Lying to me. After I gave you chances to talk to me. After I trusted you." I collapse to one knee, gasping. Blood hits the ice in little red splatters. The team's frozen, no one moving.

"And this—" Connor growls, grabbing the front of my jersey, "this is for Lexi, Avery and every other girl you've fucked over. For hurting the best fucking thing you ever had. You don't get to break every girl that gives a shit about you and walk away like it's nothing." Punch. I hit the ice hard, back thudding against the cold.

"What the fuck is happening?!" James's voice cuts through everything like a blade. Skates thunder across the rink.

My dad's there in seconds, ripping Connor off me, arms wrapped around his chest as Connor still tries to lunge, growling like a man possessed.

"Enough!" James barks, wrestling him back. "Connor—stand down. Now."

Connor's chest heaves. His fists are still clenched, knuckles bloody. His glare burns down at me like I'm something he needs to scrape off his skate blade.

"She's my sister, Coach," he snarls, voice shaking. "And he's a fucking liar."

I look up at him, dazed and stunned. "What?" I breathe.

No one answers. James's face is thunderous. "We do this in the locker room. Now." But Connor just stares at me.

Hurt, rage, betrayal—all wrapped into one look I've never seen from him before. "She trusted you," he says quietly. "And you fucking broke her. Now shes walked away, shes gone."

My heart stops cold. "What do you mean walk away—?" He skates off without answering.

And suddenly, I can't feel my legs.

The silence in the locker room is *deafening*.

I'm slumped on the bench, jersey halfway off, blood crusting under my nose, jaw already swelling.

Connor's across the room, pacing like he's seconds from exploding. Shoulders rigid, knuckles split. He hasn't looked at me once since we walked in.

James storms in behind us, door slamming so hard the walls shake.

"Sit," he barks at Connor.

Connor doesn't even flinch.

"I said *sit*."

He finally drops onto the bench like it's the hardest thing he's done all day, but his fists stay clenched, like his body hasn't gotten the memo that this round's over.

James rounds on him first, voice sharp and low. "You just assaulted your own teammate in front of everyone. You better give me a goddamn good reason."

Connor doesn't even hesitate. "He lied to me."

"About what?"

His eyes snap to mine. No hesitation now. Just rage.

"Him and my sister."

James blinks. "What?"

Connor stands again, voice rising. "They've been sneaking around for weeks. Maybe longer. He let me go on, saying how I didn't want any of the guys near her, how I needed her to be okay—and he just sat there. Didn't say a fucking word."

James turns to me slowly. "Is this true?"

My stomach turns, but I nod. "Yeah. It's true."

Connor laughs. Bitter. Like it tastes bad coming out. "Fucking hell. At least you're admitting it now."

James mutters something under his breath, but Connor keeps going.

"And you know what really gets me?" he says, louder now. "I gave you the chance to come clean. Multiple times.

But you kept lying. You just kept lying, like you didn't owe me a damn thing."

I shift forward on the bench. "I didn't want to lie to you—"

"*Bullshit.*" Connor lunges again. James throws an arm across his chest to stop him.

"You're a liar," Connor seethes, eyes wild. "I saw you. At the party. With those girls all over you. *Flirting.* Smirking like she didn't even exist."

"I wasn't flirting—Connor, I *left*. I didn't touch them."

"You didn't come *home*," he spits. "She noticed. You left her there thinking you picked someone fucking puck bunny over her. You know her ex cheated on her, he fucking ruined her and then you go and do this to her. Make her think shes important to you, have her sneak around behind my back and then drop her as soon as something shinier comes along."

I go cold.

"No. I would never hurt her! I didn't know she was even planning on leaving..."

"She was heartbroken," he snaps. "I've never seen her look like that. She thought she meant *nothing* to you."

My stomach turns to stone.

"She packed a bag. Told me not to tell you. Said she'd had enough. *Took the goddamn job in Louisiana.*" His voice cracks. "She left, Ethan. Because of *you.*"

The floor drops out from under me. I can't speak, can't move.

"You hurt one of the most important people in my life and broke our friendship in the process."

James is still holding him back, but Connor's fists are shaking like he wants nothing more than to finish what he started on the ice.

I can't speak. I can't fucking *breathe.*

Connor jerks his arms free from James's hold, storms toward the exit. Just before he leaves, he spins around and points a finger at me like he's casting a curse.

"If she never comes back, it's on you."

And then he's gone.

James doesn't say anything for a long moment. Just stands there, jaw tight, eyes narrowed.

Finally, he exhales. "Get cleaned up."

Then he walks out too.

And I'm left sitting there, bleeding, shaking, wrecked.

Because Avery's gone.

And I didn't even know she was breaking when she left.

I burst through the locker room doors, bleeding from my lip, still reeling, still raw.

Connor's halfway down the rink, throwing a puck into the net like it's a goddamn dartboard.

"*Connor!*" I shout, voice echoing off the walls. My skates slam down onto the ice. My breath fogs in the cold. "*You don't get to fucking say that to me and walk away.*"

He turns. Chest rising fast. Eyes pure fire.

"You wanna keep this going?" he growls, skating toward me. "You really think you're the fucking victim right now?"

"I didn't do anything wrong," I shout. "Not to her."

"You *lied* to me. and then hurt her"

"I didn't lie. I *protected* her. I protected us. I was protecting what ever we had between us. Neither one fo us wanted to hurt you and we was just trying to figure out what was between us. I would never hurt her!"

"You protected *yourself*," he snaps. "She was already breaking, and you showed her that you didn't give a fuck about her."

I skate closer. Blood's dripping down my chin again, but I don't care. I need him to hear this.

"I *care* about her," I shout. "More than I've cared about anything in my fucking life."

"Too late," he snarls. "You don't get to say that now. She's gone. She's fucking *gone*, and you didn't fight for her. She left thinking she was just another girl in your revolving door of bad decisions. You could have spoke to me, I would have understood, I wouldn't have stood in between real feelings. But you didn't, you just used her to pass the time. Just like all the others."

I lunge forward, chest to chest now, nose inches from his. "*I've changed.*"

Connor scoffs. "You think changing your jersey number means you're a new man?"

I shove him. "I'm not that guy anymore."

"You are right, you are fucking worse," he spits, and slams his shoulder into mine, knocking me backwards. I skid, my feet slipping, landing hard on my side with a groan.

The team floods the ice—Carter, Mason, even one of the rookies skates in between us to block any more hits.

Then—

"*Enough!*" Liam's voice cuts through the chaos like a gunshot. Everyone freezes.

Liam skates into the middle of us, eyes on Connor. "You wanna know where Ethan went after the party?"

Connor doesn't respond, just breathes hard, hands clenched, watching me bleed.

Liam steps forward. "He came home with *me.* Crashed at my place."

"What?"

"He didn't touch those girls. They tried. He said no. Told them he wasn't on the market."

Connor's face slackens—just a little.

"He sat on my couch, Connor," Liam says. "Looked like someone kicked his ribs in when he realised you two had left without him. *He didn't even know why she'd left.*"

The silence that falls is cold and heavy.

Connor looks at me. Really looks.

And I see it—that flicker of doubt. The beginning of the crack. The part of him that *wants* to believe me, but doesn't know how to let go of what he thinks he saw.

"She saw you with those puck bunnies," he mutters. "*I* saw you."

I breathe through the ache. "I was being polite. I was saying no. I told them to back off. I didn't want *anyone* else. I want Avery. It's been Avery since I first met her, and she dragged me into a cold shower. We may not have seen eye to eye all these years but that night she found me on your door step, we connected through our pain and found comfort with each other. It was easy to be with her, she made things hurt less. She has been what's kept me going this season when everyone else had wrote me off. She believed in me."

His jaw twitches. Something in his eyes flickers.

He swallows hard.

No one moves.

No one speaks.

Just the sound of the puck still clattering in the net behind him.

And all I can think is—

I let her walk away.

Because I waited too long to show her the truth.

Connor's still breathing hard, jaw tight, fists clenched like he's waiting for me to flinch or lie again.

But I don't move.

I just look at him—blood on my face, heart on the ice between us—and say the one thing I haven't yet.

"I love her."

His face twists like I just stabbed him.

I step forward, slow, careful. "I didn't plan it. I didn't want to hurt anyone. But I fucking love her, and I was going to tell you. I just... didn't want to lose you too."

He looks away. Swipes a hand across his mouth. Doesn't speak.

"I should've told you," I keep going. "From the beginning. She deserved that. You deserved that. I should have fought for what we had, even if it meant standing my ground with you."

"You're my *best friend*," he says finally, his voice cracked glass. "And she's my *sister*. I didn't want perfect, Ethan. I just wanted you to be honest."

"I know." My voice is barely there. "And I wasn't. I was scared."

He laughs. It's bitter. Hollow. "You, scared of me? That's new."

"I was scared of fucking it all up," I say. "Of losing everything. You. Her. This team. I've spent months trying to *be better*, and the second I felt something real, I panicked."

Connor finally looks at me again. His expression isn't anger anymore—it's disappointment. Pain.

"You didn't fuck it up by loving her," he says. "You fucked it up by making her think she didn't matter."

"I know," I say. "And I swear to God, if I ever get the chance again, I won't make the same mistake."

He watches me for a long time. Then—finally—his shoulders drop. Just a little.

"Do you even know where she went?"

"No." My throat tightens. "I didn't know she was going. I didn't even get to tell her how I feel."

Something in his face softens.

"She flew out this morning," he says quietly. "Louisiana. Dan lined up a hotel for her last night. She said she didn't want you to know."

Fuck.

My chest caves. I stare down at the ice, jaw clenched hard enough to ache.

"I really lost her."

Connor exhales. Steps closer. Then, after a pause, he mutters, "You're a dumbass."

I huff a humorless breath. "Yeah. I know."

"And I'm still pissed at you."

"I know that too."

"But..." He rubs the back of his neck. "If you meant all that—if you really didn't touch anyone else, if you meant it when you said you love her—then maybe..."

He trails off.

I look up. "Maybe what?"

He shrugs. "Maybe there's still time to fix it. Maybe she's not gone for good."

I blink.

And for the first time since I hit the ice this morning, I feel the tiniest flicker of hope.

"You'd let me try?"

Connor groans. "Don't make it weird. I'm not giving you my blessing. I'm just... not gonna break your nose again today."

I manage a smile. Bloody. Crooked. Honest. "That's the nicest thing you've ever said to me."

He flips me off and turns back toward the locker room. "Get your shit together, Wilson. And hurry the fuck up. She doesn't wait around."

I don't waste a second.

Chapter 27

The airport is loud in the way only airports can be—babies crying, suitcases dragging, voices muffled under announcements and the low thrum of planes taxiing outside. But all I hear is my own heartbeat.

I sit at Gate B17, hoodie pulled up, legs crossed, backpack at my feet, like this is just another flight. Another trip. Like I'm not actively bleeding out behind my ribs.

The gate attendant calls for boarding. Group Three.

That's me.

I pull out my phone. One last message to the girls.

To: Group Chat - GIRLS

Avery:

Love you all. Boarding now. Don't respond—I'm turning off my phone.

Thanks for everything, I'll message when I get there.

Then, separately, I text Connor.

To: Connor

Thank you for being my safe place. I'll message you when I land. Please don't hate him. Or me.

I stare at the messages for a second longer than I should.

Then I switch the phone off. Just like that.

Silence.

My stomach flips as I stand. My feet feel heavier than they should. I hand over my boarding pass with a smile that doesn't reach my eyes and walk through the jet bridge like I'm doing the right thing. Like I haven't spent every second since that night wondering what *might've* happened if I'd just waited a little longer. If I'd stayed.

But I can't think like that. I made my decision.

And it's too late now.

I find my seat. Middle row. No window. No distractions. No chance of escape. My bag goes under the seat in front of me, and my heart goes somewhere I won't be able to reach for a while.

The flight attendant drones through the safety speech, but I don't hear a word. All I can think about is the way he looked at me. The way his hands held my waist like I was something precious. The way I told myself not to fall for him.

And fell anyway.

The plane starts to taxi. Then accelerate. Then lift.

And I break.

Silently.

Face turned to the side. Hoodie hiding my eyes. Shoulders shaking so subtly no one notices.

But my heart knows. My heart *feels* it.

Because this?

This is the first time I've ever left somewhere and felt like I was leaving *home*.

Louisiana air is different.

Thicker somehow. Warmer. Smells like humidity and palm trees and too many fresh starts.

I step out of the airport in a fog, dragging my suitcase behind me like it weighs more than just clothes. It's early afternoon—the sun's already brutal overhead, and my hoodie feels suffocating. But I don't take it off.

I don't feel ready to let the world see me yet.

The taxi driver loads my bag into the trunk and asks where I'm headed.

I tell him the address Dan sent. The temporary apartment just a few miles from the stables. "It's a month-to-month rental," Dan had said. "Enough to get your bearings before they move you into staff housing."

It feels like a punishment. Like purgatory in pastel.

I slide into the backseat, roll down the window a crack, and pull out my phone.

It takes a moment to boot up.

Then it lights up.

And everything inside me freezes.

31 missed calls.

14 from Ethan.

8 from Connor.

The rest from Liam, Carter, even fucking Mason.

There are texts too.

Pages of them.

A missed FaceTime from Lexi.

A voice note from Maya.

I stare at the screen like it's a bomb about to detonate. My thumb hovers over Ethan's name, heart stuttering in my chest.

Then I finally open his first message.

Ethan:

Please don't get on that flight.

You don't understand what happened.

I need to see you.
We need to talk.
Avery, please.

Another one, a few minutes later.
Ethan:
I didn't go home with anyone. I swear. I told those girls I wasn't interested. I tried to find you. I waited.

Then—
Ethan (2:13 a.m.):
I didn't know you were leaving. I didn't know you thought... fuck. Please, I'm begging you. Call me. Text me. Anything.

I close my eyes and let my head fall back against the seat.

The cab rolls on. Sunshine beams through the window. My phone buzzes again in my hand—another message.

From Connor.

Connor:
I owe you an apology. A big one.
I didn't know the truth. I do now.
He loves you, Ave.
Don't hate him for being late to say it.

My throat closes.

I scroll through the unread messages like a ghost. My eyes sting, but I don't cry. I already did that somewhere over Georgia.

The taxi pulls into a quiet complex. Stucco walls. Palm trees. A community pool that smells like chlorine and loneliness.

The driver gets my bag. I pay him, tip generously, thank him with a voice that's barely there.

And then I just stand there.

Suitcase by my side.

Phone burning in my hand.

Messages I'm too scared to answer.

Memories I can't run from, no matter how many miles I put between us.

I thought leaving would help.

But now?

Now I don't know what the hell I was thinking.

Because Louisiana might have palm trees.

But it doesn't have him.

The sun is setting outside the little apartment window, painting everything in soft gold like it's trying to make me believe this was the right choice.

My suitcase is unpacked. My new boots are lined up by the door. There's a training schedule on the counter, already smudged with coffee. I'm here. I've landed. I'm supposed to be starting over.

So why does it still feel like something's broken?

I stare at my phone for too long before I finally tap *Call.*

Connor picks up on the second ring. "Avery?"

His voice sounds cautious. Like he doesn't know if I'm calling to scream or sob.

"Hey," I say softly. "I just... I needed to talk to you."

Silence stretches for a moment before he breathes out. "You okay?"

"I will be," I say. And then I press the heel of my palm against my eye because I'm not ready to cry again. "This move... I need it. I need a fresh start. Not because I'm running from everything—but because I'm choosing myself for once."

Connor's quiet.

"I don't need to know everything," I continue, voice trembling just a little. "I don't need the timeline or the explanations. I just know how I felt. I know what I saw. And I know how much it hurt to think he didn't care."

"Avery—"

"I care about him, okay?" I whisper. "I *do*. But I can't build my life around a guy. Not even one I thought maybe... maybe I could've had something real with."

There's a crack in my voice on that last line, and Connor hears it. I know he does.

"I get it," he says finally, and it sounds like it hurts him too. "I do. You deserve something solid. You deserve to feel chosen every damn day, not just when it's convenient."

I sniff. "Thanks."

"I love you, Ave. So fucking much. I'm proud of you for doing what you need, even if it sucks that you had to go."

I nod, even though he can't see it. "I'll stay in touch. I promise."

"You better," he says, but it's gentle. "You call me anytime. Day or night."

"I will." I pause, then exhale slowly. "Can you... tell Ethan to let me have this space? I need to figure things out without hearing his voice every time my phone buzzes."

Connor hesitates. "He didn't do anything, Ave. I swear to you. He—"

"No," I interrupt, quickly. Too fast. "Please. I just need to do this for me. I need to put myself first for a change."

I hear something in the background then—a door, a voice.

Familiar. Wrecked.

Ethan.

"Avery?" His voice is faint. "Is she—can I—please, let me just—"

My heart implodes.

"No, I—I have to go," I say, panic rushing in like a tidal wave. "Tell him I'm okay. Just... not ready."

"Ave—"

"Bye, Connor," I whisper, and hang up before I can change my mind. Before I can hear another second of his voice and fall apart all over again.

The phone slides from my hand and hits the couch cushion with a dull thud.

I sit there in the fading light, wrapped in silence.

Hurting.

Healing.

Trying to believe I'm doing the right thing.

Even if it feels like it's breaking me in half.

Chapter 28

Avery

Louisiana – Week One

The first time I sit on *Revelation*, I swear I forget everything.

Every worry. Every ache. Every stupid heartbreak I packed with me like emotional carry-on.

He's seventeen hands of muscle, precision, and ego. A dark bay stallion with a white slash down his face and eyes that scream *don't fuck with me*—and I love him instantly.

"You'll need to earn his trust," Dan says, watching from the rail. "But once he gives it, you'll never ride anything like him again."

He's not wrong.

Rev is powerful, cocky, a living freight train of impulsive brilliance—and I'm laughing the first time he explodes into a clean flying lead change like it's nothing. My heart *soars*. My blood sings. And I remember why I fought so hard for this career in the first place.

Here, in the arena, everything makes sense.

My body moves without thought, my mind clears, and I feel like *me* again. Not the scandal. Not the sob story. Not the girl who fell for the wrong guy and fled the fallout.

Just Avery Maddox—rider, trainer, fighter.

But the high doesn't last.

Not once I'm back in the barn, stripping tack and brushing sweat from Rev's sleek, shimmering coat.

Because my phone buzzes again.

And like clockwork... it's him.

Ethan

Hey. Hope the new place is still treating you right. I miss you.

I stare at the message longer than I mean to.

Then I set the phone down on the stable bench and walk away.

Ten minutes later, I come back and read it again.

Every morning starts the same.

Feed. Muck. Ride.

And every morning, another message.

Ethan

Morning, Red. Hope today is full of good horses and even better coffee. You deserve both.

I roll my eyes and read it again.

Three days in, Rev bucks me clean off mid-warmup.

I hit the ground hard, flat on my back, wind gone.

Dan runs over, but I'm already laughing. Not from adrenaline—just disbelief. Because as I sit up and rub my spine, I realize I *miss* this. The pain. The challenge. The proof that I'm alive.

And then, like clockwork, my phone buzzes in my jacket pocket.

Ethan

I had a dream last night you were teaching a horse to salsa dance. You were yelling at it in Spanish. Not sure what you're feeding them down there but I think you're a witch.

I don't laugh. I *should*, but I don't.

Instead, I pull my knees to my chest and stare at the empty arena, feeling more alone than ever.

Because for the first time since I got here, I want to tell someone how good I'm doing. How wild Rev is. How proud I am of the progress I've already made.

But I can't.

Because the only person I want to tell is the one I left behind.

By midweek, I've won over half the barn—including a cantankerous mare named Clementine who won't let anyone else clean her feet. I'm being offered more ride time, more responsibility. There's talk of prepping two mounts for competition under my name.

It's everything I ever wanted.

And I'm still waking up hollow.

Still checking my phone like an addict.

Still reading every text before I throw the phone across the bed like it personally betrayed me.

Ethan

You looked amazing in that video Dan posted. I know you might not be reading these, but I'm proud of you anyway. You're magic.

I cry for twenty straight minutes after that one.

Then I ride Rev like we've both got something to prove.

We fly.

Friday night, I sit on the stable roof with a beer and the kind of exhaustion that sinks into your bones.

The stars here are different—cleaner, sharper. The kind that whisper you're small but still part of something.

My phone buzzes in my lap.

Ethan
I miss you.

No pretense. No jokes.
　Just three words.
　Tears start falling.
　Because I miss him too.
　More than I should.
　More than I can admit.
　And maybe I'm healing. Maybe I'm strong. Maybe I'm doing the brave thing by chasing my own life and standing on my own feet.
　But I've never felt lonelier in my life.

Chapter 29

Ethan

I haven't texted her yet this morning.

Not because I forgot.

Because I'm trying to give her what she asked for.

Space.

It's the hardest thing I've ever done.

Liam tosses me a water bottle across the locker room. "You heading out with us after practice?"

I shake my head. "Nah. Got plans."

"Lemme guess," Carter chimes in. "Sit on your couch, scroll through instagram looking for videos of Avery riding, and stare at your phone until you fall asleep?"

"Basically," I mutter, pulling on my hoodie.

He shrugs. "Honestly? Kind of love that for you."

Connor walks in just then, towel around his neck, post-skate and flushed with effort. He freezes for half a second—like he's bracing for something—but then he nods at me.

And it's not stiff. Not forced.

Just... real.

"You good?" he asks.

I nod. "Getting there."

He grabs a protein bar off the shelf, tosses it to me. "You've been solid lately. On and off the ice."

"Trying."

"You're doing more than trying," Liam says, stepping in with his usual half-grin. "You've done what none of us thought you'd do—put someone else first."

That lands harder than I expect.

Because it's true. I wanted to chase her. To drop everything and fly to Louisiana and *fight*. But when she asked for space? I gave it.

Even when it gutted me.

Connor sits beside me on the bench. For a second, he doesn't say anything. Then he sighs.

"She's doing okay," he says quietly. "Sent me a video of one of the horses she's working with. You'd love him. Asshole attitude, big heart, kicks like a freight train."

I laugh under my breath. "Sounds familiar."

He cracks a smile. "She didn't want me to tell you. But I figured you'd want to know she's safe."

"Thanks, man."

There's a long pause.

Then—he adds, "I didn't think you had it in you."

"To what? Not be a selfish prick?"

"To wait," he says. "To respect her enough to let her figure it out without pressure."

I rub a hand over my jaw, heart twisting.

"I just want her to come back because she wants to," I say. "Not because I begged. Not because she felt guilty. Just... because she chooses me."

Carter whistles from across the room. "Holy *character development*, Batman."

Liam nods solemnly. "I'm honestly proud of you, dude. This is some Grade-A pining. Slow-burn, emotional-wreckage, main-character energy."

"I'm living in a goddamn Nicholas Sparks novel," I grumble.

"More like a Taylor Swift bridge," Carter mutters. "But yeah."

Connor stands, claps a hand on my shoulder, and for the first time in weeks—maybe months—I feel like we're brothers again.

"She'll come back when she's ready," he says.

I nod.

"And if she doesn't?"

I exhale slowly. "Then I'll still be proud of her. Always."

He looks at me for a long beat.

Then says, "Let me know when you're ready to do something about it."

And just like that, the idea's planted.

Maybe space is good. Maybe patience is noble.

But maybe—just *maybe*—it's time to stop bleeding quietly.

And fight for her the *right* way.

One month later

The lads all burst though my door at 5:43am. And my plan is in fully swing.

I'm about to willingly get on a flight *to* Louisiana.

To watch *Avery*.

Compete.

No one told her. Obviously. Because *surprise emotional ambush* is the love language of this group.

"She's gonna freak out," I mutter, stuffing a hoodie into my bag as Liam lounges on my new couch like he paid rent.

"In a good way," Connor says from the doorway, arms crossed, that weird proud-big-brother energy dialed up to eleven. "She needs to see you."

I glance at him. "You sure about this?"

He shrugs. "You didn't chase her when she left. You respected her. You waited. Now? I think it's time."

"I'm not showing up to win her back," I say, even though every cell in my body is screaming *yes you are*. "I just want to see her ride. Cheer her on. Let her know I'm still here And I'm so proud of her."

Connor's mouth tugs up. "Then let's go cheer."

Ten hours later we're at the airport, half the team in tow.

Lexi, Maya, and Rachel show up like it's the *Met Gala of revenge support*. Rachel's got sunglasses on indoors. Maya's carrying travel snacks like a saint. Lexi? Lexi is on a mission.

"Tell me we're wearing coordinated outfits," she says as we hit security. "Because I've got a hoodie that says 'Team Avery' and I *will* make it everyone's problem."

"No coordinated anything," I say. "We're going for subtle."

"You... Subtle?" Rachel mutters. "Subtle left the building months ago."

We clear TSA. Grab overpriced coffees. I'm half-listening to Liam and Carter arguing about middle seats when Connor nudges my shoulder.

"Hey," he says. "You know I meant it earlier—about being proud."

I glance over.

He nods, serious now. "You've changed, man. Apartment's been quiet without you. Weird."

I smirk. "You've been begging for me to move out since I left protein powder in your Vitamix. And my new place is around the corner from you."

"Yeah, well." He shrugs. "Didn't think I'd *miss* you being in my face all the time."

"Don't get emotional on me now," I say, but my chest is tight in that stupid nostalgic way.

He chuckles. "Just don't fuck this up. Okay?"

"Not planning to."

Boarding starts.

I sling my bag over my shoulder and head toward the gate.

Lexi falls into step beside me. "She has no idea we're coming, does she?"

"Nope."

She grins. "Good."

We scan our passes, start down the jet bridge.

Just before we step onto the plane, Lexi grabs my arm.

I turn.

She looks at me—really *looks* at me. Her voice softens. "I'm proud of you."

I blink. "You just said that when I didn't trip over my suitcase fifteen minutes ago."

"No." Her smile's different now. "I mean it. You're not the guy I met all those years ago. Back then? You were fire and chaos and heartbreak. But now?" She exhales. "I finally see what it looks like when you love someone. And I'm so fucking glad it's her."

My throat tightens.

"Thanks, Lex."

She pats my chest. "Now don't cry on the plane, Romeo. You'll freak out the flight attendants."

I shake my head, laughing, and follow her into the cabin, heart pounding like I'm on my way to the biggest game of my life.

Which, honestly?

I might be.

Because this time, the win isn't a goal.

It's *her*.

I don't think I've blinked since we got here.

The arena is massive—white fences, green fields, an endless expanse of sunshine and perfectly groomed horses that cost more than my car. There's an actual *jumbotron* with event names cycling through. And everywhere I look, it's boots, breeches, helmets, and energy drinks.

Connor whistles low beside me. "This is... legit."

Lexi's filming the whole thing like we're on a documentary. "I feel like I should be whispering commentary like it's the Olympics."

Rachel's already halfway to the concession stand for overpriced pretzels and gossip.

Me? I'm locked in. Eyes scanning every rider, every bay and chestnut blur of motion.

Waiting.

Because somewhere in this sea of horsepower and spandex is *her*.

Avery Maddox. Wearing my number in her heart even if I can't see it on her back anymore.

"Got her," Maya says, pointing toward the warm-up ring.

My breath stalls.

She's there—helmet on, auburn hair pulled tight, hands firm on the reins of the biggest damn horse I've ever seen. The thing looks like it was carved out of stone and taught how to fly.

She's poised. Focused. Sitting tall in the saddle like she's part of the beast beneath her. Her heels down, eyes ahead, perfect posture, complete control.

And fuck, she looks good.

Not just beautiful. Not just confident.

She looks *happy*.

Something deep in my chest twists. Because yeah—I'm proud. Insanely proud.

But I also miss her like hell.

"Damn," Carter murmurs. "She looks like she owns the place."

"She *does*," Connor says quietly.

Avery doesn't see us. Not yet.

She's laser-focused as the horse moves into a canter—controlled, powerful. They take a few practice jumps like it's nothing. Effortless. She pats his neck afterward, and I swear I see the grin even from across the ring.

She's glowing.

And I've never wanted to be part of someone's life more than I want to be part of *hers*.

The announcer's voice crackles through the speakers. "Next in the arena: Avery Maddox, riding Titan, representing Meadow Ridge Stables."

My whole body tenses.

This is it.

We rush toward the edge of the arena, weaving through parents and trainers and a few terrifying nine-year-olds with Olympic-level energy. We find a spot along the fence, hearts pounding, collectively holding our breath.

Then she enters the ring.

And holy *shit*.

Titan eats up the space like it's nothing. Avery sits like she was born in that saddle. They soar over the first fence—clean, powerful. The crowd claps. My hands grip the top rail like I'm watching her ride straight through my ribcage.

"She's incredible," Lexi whispers.

"Yeah," I say. "She always was."

Every jump is sharper than the last—tight turns, perfect landings, not a single rail knocked. She's in the zone. You can see it in her face. Focused. Fierce.

And when she clears the final jump with a clean round and throws her hand in the air with a whoop of triumph?

The team erupts like we just won the Cup.

"THAT'S OUR GIRL!" Rachel yells, waving a foam finger she definitely wasn't supposed to bring.

"She has *no* idea we're here," Liam grins.

"She's about to," I murmur, heart pounding.

Because as Avery slows Titan to a trot, circling toward the exit gate, her eyes scan the crowd—smiling, breathless, buzzing from the ride.

And then she sees us.

Me.

Her gaze lands on mine like a fucking earthquake.

She freezes in the saddle.

Eyes wide. Chest heaving. Jaw slack.

And for the first time since she walked away from me, I see it—that spark of something raw and hopeful and terrified all at once.

I just smile at her.

And she doesn't move.

Not until Titan flicks an ear and nudges forward again.

Avery finally blinks.

And all I can do is wait—still on the edge of the fence, every breath locked in my throat—hoping this moment is the start of something new.

Or at least the end of her silence.

Chapter 30

Avery

Titan's still dancing beneath me, full of adrenaline and muscle and pride, and I'm laughing—actually laughing—because we *nailed* that round. Clean. Fast. No rails.

I can hear Dan's voice somewhere beyond the gate yelling, "Hell yeah, Maddox!" And it's all hitting me at once: the wind in my face, the sunlight on my back, the smell of grass and horse sweat and sweet, stupid freedom.

This is what I've worked for.

And for one perfect moment, it feels like enough.

I glance toward the crowd, searching for Dan's clipboard and over-caffeinated smirk—and that's when I see them.

No.

No, no, *no.*

I blink once.

Then again.

My body goes cold and hot all at once, like my brain's lagging five seconds behind my eyes.

Because standing at the edge of the ring, like something out of a dream or a delusion I haven't let myself have in weeks—

Is *Ethan*.

And not just him.

All of them.

Connor, Liam, Lexi, Maya, Rachel—my people. My chaos crew. My uninvited, apparently-airborne emotional support system.

They're cheering. Laughing. Lexi's waving like a crazy person like we're not in the middle of an international damn event. Connor's got his arms crossed but his mouth is twitching. Liam's got a giant sign that just says "GO AVERY (PLZ DON'T FALL)" in shaky marker.

But Ethan...

He's not doing anything flashy.

Just standing there.

Watching me like I'm the only person in the arena. Like he flew all this way just to *see* me.

He raises a hand.

Just a wave.

Casual. Small. Devastating.

And it hits me so hard I forget to breathe.

Titan slows. I blink again, disoriented, chest suddenly tight.

Because I haven't seen him in weeks.

Haven't *heard* him, except through those quiet texts I've tried so hard not to answer. The ones that hit like sucker punches every time I read them under the covers before bed.

Morning, Aves. You're probably already out there killing it. Just wanted you to know I'm still thinking about you.

Night, Maddox. Still proud of you. Still here.

I don't need you to answer. Just need you to know I haven't gone anywhere.

And now here he is.

He came.

And I have no idea what to do with that.

Titan bumps the gate gently, reminding me we're still moving, still here. My hands are trembling on the reins now. My pulse won't slow. I try to keep my head up, try to ride off like a professional—but I feel *wrecked.*

Wrecked in a way that feels dangerously close to hope.

Dan meets me just outside the gate, handing off a bottle of water with a grin. "Kid, that was flawless. If you don't podium today, I'll personally fight the judges."

I try to smile back. I do. But it comes out shaky.

"You okay?" he asks, frowning now. "You look like you've seen a ghost."

"No," I croak. "Not a ghost."

I glance back at the stands, where the team is still gathered.

Where *he's* still standing.

"I just wasn't expecting... them."

Dan follows my gaze. His eyebrows lift. "Friends?"

I nod slowly.

"One of them more than the others?"

My throat burns. "Yeah."

Dan doesn't press. Just pats Titan's flank and gives me a gentle nod. "Take a walk. Cool him out. Then go say hi."

"I don't know if I can."

He gives me a look. "You can handle a half ton animal. You can handle a few people who love you."

I click my tongue and guide Titan toward the cool down trail.

But even as we walk, my hands are still shaking.

Because I don't know what Ethan's going to say.

I don't know what *I'm* going to say.

All I know is—he came.

He came without asking.

Without needing an answer.

And suddenly, I'm not sure I can keep pretending that doesn't mean something.

I walk Titan in slow circles behind the stables, one hand resting on his shoulder, the other gripping the lead rope tighter than necessary. My thoughts won't slow down. I try to focus on the rhythm of his steps, the feel of the leather in my hand, the warmth of his side.

But I can't shake it.

They're here.

He's here.

And suddenly everything I've been holding together for weeks feels fragile.

Titan lets out a breath, nudges my arm. I scratch his neck without thinking. He knows he did well. The round was clean. Precise. Better than anything I've ridden in months. And for a few minutes after we crossed that finish line, I actually felt good.

But now?

Now it's all crashing back in.

He came.

Not just to see me—but for me. I can feel that truth crawling up the back of my throat and I don't know what to do with it.

I was supposed to be past this. I was supposed to have moved on. Focused on my career. On building something that didn't depend on him being a part of it.

I don't know how to hold that line anymore.

My phone buzzes in my pocket.

I know who it is before I check.

So proud of you. You are fucking magic.

I don't realize I'm crying until Titan shifts and snorts, catching the edge of my sleeve. I wipe my cheek with the back of my hand and shake my head.

"Sorry," I whisper. "I'm supposed to be stronger than this."

I lead him into his stall, brush him down with slow, even strokes. I try not to think about how close they all are—just a few dozen feet from where I'm standing. I try not to think about the way Ethan looked at me the night I left. Or the way he touched me like I was something he couldn't bear to lose.

I try.

And then I hear them.

"Avery!"

Rachel's voice hits me before anything else. Loud, clear, no hesitation.

"Back here," I call, voice barely steady.

She rounds the corner first—arms already outstretched, followed by Lexi, Maya, and Connor trailing behind them. Lexi's mid-bite on a protein bar and already smiling like she knows I'm about to fall apart. Maya's quiet but alert, her eyes locked on me. And Connor—he doesn't say anything yet. Just gives me a look that settles something in my chest.

Rachel reaches me first. She doesn't wait. She throws her arms around me and hugs like she means it. Full pressure, no holding back. My spine pops.

I don't care.

"You were unreal," she says. "I wanted to scream but Connor threatened to confiscate my voice box."

I laugh. Just barely.

Lexi hugs me next—warm and solid and steady.

"You looked like you were meant to be out there."

Maya nods, pulling me in quickly. "You did what people wait their whole lives to do."

I look between them, blinking hard. "You guys came?"

Lexi tosses her wrapper in my tack box. "Of course we did."

"But you didn't tell me."

Rachel glances at Connor. "Someone wanted it to be a surprise."

Connor steps forward and hugs me too. No words. Just grounding. Familiar. The only person who's ever really known how to anchor me.

He pulls back, rests his hands on my shoulders. "He brought us. All of us. Booked the flights. Texted the schedule. Told us we weren't allowed to distract you before the round."

My chest twists.

"He wanted to be here for you," Connor adds. "He couldn't stand the idea of you looking up and not seeing anyone you loved in the crowd."

Before I can respond, I hear footsteps behind me.

I turn.

It's him.

Ethan stands at the edge of the stall. Hands in his pockets. Shoulders set like he's trying not to break his own rules. His eyes are on me and no one else.

Lexi clears her throat. Loudly. "We're going to give you two some air."

Rachel grabs Maya's sleeve. "Come on. I think I saw a coffee stand."

Connor holds my gaze one last time. Then follows them.

It's just us.

Ethan doesn't move.

Neither do I.

His eyes don't leave mine.

When he finally speaks, it's quiet.

"I didn't touch them."

I blink. "What?"

"The girls. That night. After the party. I didn't hook up with anyone."

He takes a step forward.

"I went to Liam's. I didn't even know you were gone until the next morning. And when Connor told me what you thought—Avery, never wanted you to feel second best."

I try to speak. I can't.

"I didn't want you to leave."

"I left because I had to," I whisper. "Not because I didn't want you. But because I needed to prove I could want something for myself. That I could choose a path without looking over my shoulder to see if someone else approved of it. I did it for me."

Ethan nods slowly. "You were right to go. I am so proud of you for what you have achieved out here. I want you to follow your dreams. But I also want to be apart of your life."

I step closer. Just once.

"I was scared," I admit. "You were the one thing I let in. And then I left, thinking it was strength. But it felt like I tore something out of my own chest."

He closes the distance between us. Not touching, not rushing.

"I wasn't ready before," he says. "But I am now. And I'm not asking for a second chance because I think I deserve one—I'm asking because I'm willing to work for it. For you."

"I don't know what happens next."

"I do," he says. "I keep showing up. You keep doing what you love. And maybe... maybe we figure out how to let ourselves have both."

My throat tightens.

"I can't be the thing you run to when you're falling apart."

"You're not," he says. "You're the reason I'm trying to stay whole."

That's it.

My forehead hits his chest. His arms wrap around me, strong and sure. His hand settles between my shoulder blades. His breath hitches when I press closer.

He doesn't kiss me.

I don't ask him to.

But standing there in the quiet, the weight of everything between us slowly lifting, I realize I'm not scared anymore.

This isn't the end.

And maybe—for the first time in a long time—

It's not about proving anything.

It's just about finding my way back to him.

The applause is deafening.

I barely hear my name over the sound of it.

"Avery Maddox and Titan—takes **first place!**"

My heart slams into my ribs.

Then the announcer adds it—calm, professional, but unmistakable:

"And with that ride, Avery Maddox walks away with this year's Grand Classic title and a prize purse of **£150,000**."

The crowd *erupts*.

The world tilts.

My vision blurs—not with tears, not yet—but with the kind of disbelieving high that only comes when the dream you've been clawing toward finally, finally lands in your hands.

Titan tosses his head beneath me, still humming with energy, and I lean forward, burying a hand in his mane.

"We did it," I whisper against the thunder of the crowd. "We actually fucking did it."

The whole ring feels like it's vibrating with joy— champagne popping somewhere behind the judges' booth, people cheering my name, waving, reaching toward the edge of the arena like they want to touch the moment itself.

I don't even register when the girls start running toward the barrier.

Not until Lexi screams, "You beautiful, *lethal* legend!"

Rachel's sobbing into a foam finger.

Maya's smiling like the sun cracked through her chest.

And Ethan?

Ethan is standing a little behind them.

Still.

Watching me like I just broke the sky open and redefined what light means.

His smile is small, but his eyes say everything.

Pride. Awe. *Love.*

I can't look at him for more than a second. If I do, I might shatter.

Because this is *my* win. My career. My life.

And somehow, it still doesn't feel complete without him.

I swing down from Titan and hand the reins to his groom. My legs are shaking, knees jelly, adrenaline still flooding every cell.

Someone tries to shove a bouquet into my hands. Another person grabs my arm and says, "Photos, please—over here!"

I smile. I nod. I pose. But before Titan walks off I give him a big pat and a kiss. I couldn't have done this without him.

A few minutes later, a medal gets slipped around my neck.

A massive check is held up behind me.

Cameras flash. Champagne is sprayed.

And all I can think about is the ache in my chest that money won't fix.

Because I won.

I did.

And yet somehow, I'm still holding back tears.

The lights are low.

The music is loud.

And the champagne is endless.

The afterparty is in full swing—bodies moving, voices raised, glittering glasses clinking together in chaotic harmony. Someone's wearing a cowboy hat that definitely doesn't belong to them, Rachel's trying to ride Lexi like a victory pony, and Maya is currently holding a full-on TED Talk about tequila to a poor stranger who didn't ask.

And me?

I'm on the edge of it all, drink in hand, laughing so hard my ribs hurt.

Across the room, Ethan and Connor are arm-wrestling on a barrel table that looks like it's seconds from collapse.

Connor's grinning, face flushed from beer and adrenaline. "Come on, you soft bastard. You gonna let me win just because I didn't *actually* kill you last week?"

Ethan smirks, bracing himself. "You say that like it wasn't a close call."

"You *broke* a rib," Connor says, shaking his head. "And *you* still look smug."

"I'm smug because I didn't die," Ethan fires back. "Which is honestly the bar these days."

The guys laugh.

Hard.

And for the first time in weeks, maybe months... they're just *them* again.

No tension. No fights. No sisters being secretly fucked behind closed doors.

Just Ethan and Connor. Teammates. Best friends. Idiots.

I sip my drink and let the warmth of it settle deep in my chest.

This is the good stuff.

The messy, loud, impossible kind of night that reminds you what it's like to *live*. To be surrounded by people who know your worst and still choose to stand beside you.

Lexi flops into the chair next to me, heels dangling from her fingers, cheeks flushed with laughter. "Okay, so Rachel is trying to give Connor a lap dance, It's not something I want to watch again."

"I don't even want to know," I laugh.

"She asked him to call her 'goalie daddy,' Avery. You *do* want to know."

I choke on my drink.

Maya slides in on my other side, stealing my fries. "This is the weirdest, most emotionally chaotic group of humans I've ever been associated with."

"And yet," Lexi says, toasting, "you'd kill for any of us."

"Obviously," Maya replies.

I glance around the room—at the guys, the girls, the swirl of light and sound and laughter.

At Ethan, now standing beside Connor, both of them cheering as Carter fails epically at darts and Liam slow-dances with a mop.

And I feel it.

That strange, quiet peace that settles when you know—just for now—you're exactly where you're supposed to be.

Ethan catches my eye across the room.

Just a second.

But it's enough.

The smallest smile curves his mouth. No pressure. No demand. Just that steady, quiet affection that's been showing up in my inbox for weeks now.

I smile back.

I don't know where we're going from here.

But I know tonight? I'm not running.

Not from this. Not from him.

Lexi leans in and murmurs, "Told you this story wasn't over."

And I believe her.

Because sometimes, even in the middle of heartbreak...

You get one night that reminds you what *home* feels like.

Chapter 31

Ethan

The party's still going—music thumping, drinks spilling, someone just tried to sabre a bottle of champagne with a butter knife (spoiler: didn't work). But my eyes? They're only on her.

Avery.

She's standing near the edge of the crowd, half-lit by strings of fairy lights and moonlight, laughing at something Lexi whispered in her ear. She's wearing this soft black dress that sways every time she shifts her weight, and her smile?

God.

It's the kind that brings a man to his knees.

Not the kind you get every day. The kind you fight for.

The kind you'd wait a whole damn lifetime for.

I move through the crowd like it's instinct. Like the music fades under the sound of her laugh. Like the world is narrowing down to one girl, one night, one second of courage.

"Aves," I say quietly, tapping her hand.

She turns—and when she sees me, her face softens in that way that kills me every time. Like she still can't decide if I'm a good idea, but her heart hasn't gotten the memo yet.

"Hey," she says, smile playing at the corners of her mouth.

"Dance with me."

Her eyebrows lift. "Now?"

"It's practically midnight. Isn't that the law? One slow dance under string lights?"

She laughs, soft and sweet. "You're such a sap."

"Only for you," I murmur.

And when I offer my hand, she takes it.

We step into the middle of the room as the next song slows. Something dreamy. Timeless. The kind of thing you sway to without thinking. The kind of thing that breaks you open in the best way.

My hands settle on her waist. Hers slide up to my shoulders. Our eyes lock.

We move.

Not fast. Not flashy. Just... *together.*

And it's stupid, how good this feels. How easy. How right.

"I'm really proud of you," I say into her ear, just loud enough for her to hear. "You were unstoppable out there."

Her breath catches. "I felt unstoppable."

"You looked like you belonged."

She leans her head on my shoulder, just for a second, and I swear to God, I feel something in my chest realign. Like maybe, just maybe, this isn't the ending. Maybe this is the rebuild. The quiet middle.

I tilt my head down and press my lips to her forehead. Soft. Still. Like a promise I haven't said yet.

And when she looks up at me—eyes glossy, lips parted—I kiss her.

Right there. In the middle of the party. Wrapped in fairy lights and music and everything we're too scared to say yet.

It's not rushed.

Not desperate.

Just *ours*.

We stay there, wrapped in each other like the rest of the world doesn't exist.

Until—

"FINALLY," Rachel shouts from the sidelines.

"Oh my God, this took *forever*," Lexi groans.

"Can we *please* all start betting on their breakups? Because that's the only way I'm making rent this month," Liam adds.

I break the kiss, forehead pressed to Avery's, laughing breathlessly.

She giggles, shaking her head. "We are so bad at subtle."

"No," I say. "We're bad at timing. But perfect at this."

The next second, we're surrounded—Connor leading the charge with two drinks in hand, Maya pulling Lexi into some chaotic line dance, Rachel already dragging Carter into a pretend tango.

And just like that, we're all dancing.

All laughing.

One mess of limbs and chaos and joy and everything we almost lost—but didn't.

Because somehow, against the odds, we made it back to each other.

I don't remember leaving the party.

One minute, Avery was laughing into my chest, her arms looped around my neck like she was exactly where she belonged—and the next, we were slipping out the back door like two kids about to make the worst, best decision of our lives.

The elevator doors slide shut behind us with a mechanical *ding* and the second we're alone, I'm on her.

I've waited too damn long to touch her and every second is catching up all at once.

Her back hits the wall of the elevator with a *thud*, and I cage her in, arms braced on either side of her head.

She grabs the front of my shirt, dragging me down, and our mouths crash together like we've already fallen and there's nothing left to do but burn on the way down.

Her lips are soft and demanding. Her tongue teases mine, and I groan—low and guttural—because *fuck*, she tastes like champagne and every mistake I'd gladly make again.

I pull back just an inch, breath coming hard.

"You sure about this?" I whisper, my thumb brushing the side of her jaw.

Her eyes are molten. "I want you Ethan."

I slam the 'close door' button again like I can fast-forward time.

Her hands are already under my shirt, fingers skimming over my abs, and I feel her smile when I hiss through my teeth. "Still ridiculous," she mutters, tracing the V of muscle at my waist.

"I could say the same about you," I growl, dipping my head to her throat and nipping gently just under her ear. Her whole body shudders against mine.

The elevator jerks slightly, and I drag her hips into mine so she feels *exactly* what she's doing to me.

"I got my own room," I whisper against her skin. "Just in case."

She blinks up at me, breathless. "You really thought you had a chance tonight?"

I smirk. "No. I just hoped."

She kisses me again. Slower this time. More dangerous. Like she's carving a memory into my mouth.

The elevator dings, doors opening to my floor.

I grip her hand and lead her out, not caring that we probably look drunk on each other—because we are. Her dress is a little wrinkled, her lipstick's mostly gone, and my shirt's only half tucked.

I fumble the keycard into the door and push it open.

She steps inside first.

I follow her in and close the door behind us, knowing damn well we won't be sleeping tonight.

The second the hotel room door clicks shut, it's game over.

I grab her waist and shove her against it, mouth crashing to hers like I need her to *feel* how much I've missed her. Craved her. Ached in every quiet fucking moment since the second she walked out of my life.

Her fingers fist in my shirt, tugging it up and over my head. I help, barely getting the damn thing off before my hands are back on her—gripping, dragging, claiming. She gasps when I lift her, wrapping her legs around my waist as I carry her to the bed like she weighs nothing. She doesn't.

I drop her to the mattress and she bounces once, laughing breathlessly.

It's the most beautiful sound I've ever heard.

"You laughing at me?" I ask, crawling over her, planting a knee between her legs.

"I'm laughing because this is insane," she breathes, eyes blown wide.

"No, baby," I murmur, dragging my mouth down her neck. "But it was *inevitable*."

She moans as I kiss just below her ear, then lower, over her collarbone. My hands slide up her dress, fingers skimming over silky skin, until I find the zipper at her side.

"You wore this to torture me," I whisper.

She smirks, lips parted. "Is it working?"

I pull the zipper down with a slow, deliberate drag. "You tell me."

The dress peels off her, falling around her hips. I sit back on my heels, watching her in nothing but black lace and confidence she doesn't even realize she radiates.

"Fuck, Avery," I say, voice hoarse. "You're not real."

Her legs shift, thighs parting slightly, and I swear to God my brain short-circuits. I yank the rest of the dress off, tossing it somewhere behind me, then reach for her bra.

"Off," I growl, and she arches up so I can unclip it, my hands surprisingly steady considering the war happening in my bloodstream.

The second it's gone, I don't wait.

I dip my head and kiss the swell of her breast, tongue dragging over her nipple until it peaks under my mouth. Her breath catches. My hand cups the other, fingers rolling gently, teasing until she's arching into me, moaning my name like it's a prayer and I'm the only one who can answer it.

I kiss my way down—over ribs, over soft stomach, tracing a line lower, lower, until I reach the edge of her panties.

"You still want this?" I ask, looking up.

Her eyes are fire. "If you stop now, I'll kill you."

Grinning, I hook my fingers into the lace and slide them down—slow, watching every inch of her body like I've been starved for it. Because I *have*.

When she's bare before me, I drop to my knees at the edge of the bed and drag her legs over my shoulders.

And then?

I feast.

My tongue flicks over her clit—soft and slow. Her thighs tense around my shoulders immediately.

"Jesus, Ethan—"

I groan against her, mouth already wet with her taste, and that sound alone makes her buck. I don't stop. Don't pause. I find a rhythm and I lock into it like a man on a mission.

Her fingers grip my hair, tight and shaking. "Don't stop," she gasps. "Please—fuck—don't stop."

I suck harder, tongue dragging over her, teasing and circling and tasting until she's trembling. Whimpering. Falling apart.

She starts to fall over the edge and I don't let her freefall.

I *push* her.

Two fingers slide inside, curling just right, and her whole body bows off the mattress with a strangled cry. Her thighs clamp around my head and I hold them there, riding every wave of her orgasm like it's the only thing I've ever trained for.

She shakes. Whimpers. Screams my name like it's the only word she remembers.

And when she finally slumps back, breathing hard, hair a mess, eyes glassy?

I kiss the inside of her thigh like I've just worshiped a goddess.

Because I have.

And I'm just getting started.

I crawl up her body slow, mouth trailing kisses across her stomach, chest, neck—until I'm hovering over her, both of us breathing like we just ran a goddamn marathon.

Her skin is flushed, glowing, damp with sweat. Her hair's a halo of chaos against the pillow, and her lips? Kiss-bitten and parted just enough to show me she's not done.

Not even close.

She blinks at me—barely. Eyes glazed, pupils wide. "I can't feel my legs."

I grin. "That's the idea."

She laughs, soft and wrecked, then grabs the back of my neck and pulls me into a kiss that's all teeth and heat and hunger.

And just like that?

She flips us.

One second, I'm on top of the world. The next, I'm flat on my back and she's straddling my hips, hands on my chest like she's reclaiming territory.

And I am *so* fucking here for it.

"You think you're the only one who can drive someone crazy?" she murmurs, rolling her hips once—slow, teasing—over the very obvious proof that I'm about two seconds from losing my mind.

She leans down, hair brushing over my jaw, her lips grazing my ear.

I groan—loud, low, helpless—and her laugh is evil and perfect and *mine.*

Her hands drag down my chest, nails teasing my abs, fingers toying with the waistband of my boxers.

"Off," she whispers.

"You're bossy when you're post-orgasmic."

"I'm bossy *always*," she smirks. "Now shut up and lose the pants."

I lift my hips and she pulls them down, slow, like she wants to make a goddamn meal out of it. When she gets them off, her eyes flick down and widen—just a bit.

Then she smiles.

Cocky.

Hungry.

She leans down, straddling me again, bare and bold, and kisses me like she wants to leave bruises. Her tongue tangles with mine, her fingers curl around my length, and I nearly *fucking detonate* when she strokes once, twice, with perfect pressure.

"Aves—"

"I know," she whispers.

And then she sinks down.

My head falls back. A curse tears out of my throat. I grab her hips like I need to ground myself or lose all control.

Because *fuck*, she feels like heaven wrapped in sin.

We don't move at first. Just breathe. Shake. Shudder.

Then her hips roll—once, slow—and I feel her clench around me and I swear I black out for half a second.

She rides me like it's war. Like it's revenge. Like it's forgiveness and punishment and worship all in one.

Every movement is fire. Every breath, a benediction.

And when she leans down to kiss me again—mouth hot and needy and open—I wrap my arms around her, flip her back beneath me, and fuck her like I've been waiting my whole life for this moment.

She's already gasping when I flip her onto her back, legs tangled with mine, arms wrapped around my shoulders like she can't stand to let go.

And I'm not letting her go. Not now. Not ever.

I slam back into her, deep and perfect, and she cries out—raw, unfiltered, wrecked in a way that makes my blood turn molten.

"Ethan—" she chokes.

"I've got you," I growl, kissing the words against her throat, my hips slamming into hers in a rhythm that borders on desperate. "I'm right here. Not going anywhere."

Her nails dig into my back. Her thighs lock around my waist. And the sounds she makes—Jesus, those sounds—every single one is a knife to the gut and a balm to every broken part of me.

I lean up just enough to look at her.

Eyes closed. Lips parted. Head tilted back against the pillows, like she's offering herself up to something holy. Or hellish. And I want to be both. I want to ruin her and rebuild her in the same breath.

"Aves," I rasp, voice wrecked.

She opens her eyes—barely.

"I'm gonna come," she whispers, voice trembling.

And fuck me, that does something dangerous to me.

"Look at me," I pant. "I want to see you fall apart."

And she *does*.

She unravels beneath me, every muscle going tight, her back arching, her mouth open in a soundless cry as her orgasm hits like a wave crashing through her whole body. I keep moving, chasing my own end now, desperate, wild—

Her name's on my lips when I come. Hard. Deep. Like it's the last thing I'll ever do.

It's not gentle.

It's not neat.

It's *everything*.

We collapse together. A mess of tangled limbs, sweaty skin, and broken breaths.

My face buried in her neck. Her hand fisted in my hair. Both of us still shaking, still strung out, still so fucking *in it*.

No one talks.

No one moves.

Just the sound of our hearts pounding against each other, slowly finding their way back to steady.

Minutes pass. Or maybe hours.

I finally shift—just enough to press a kiss to her shoulder. Then another. Then another.

She hums, sleepy and raw. "You okay?"

I nod into her skin. "Never better."

She rolls to her side, bringing us face to face in the dim hotel room light.

"You're unreal," I whisper, brushing a strand of hair from her face.

She smirks, tired but smug. "You too."

I tuck her closer. "I meant what I said earlier."

She blinks at me.

"I love you Avery."

No expectations. No pressure.

Just truth.

She doesn't say it back. Not yet.

But the way she nestles into my chest? The way her fingers curl against my ribs like they belong there?

That's enough.

For now.

Because tonight, I had her back.

And for the first time since she left, I finally feel whole again.

Chapter 32

Avery

I wake up tangled in limbs and sin.

The sun's filtering through the curtains like it has the audacity to exist, and I'm sore in places that haven't been sore since my last physical therapy session. My body feels like it's been wrecked in the best possible way—and the man responsible is currently asleep with one hand on my hip and the other curled under his head like he didn't just give me five orgasms and a spiritual awakening.

Five. *FIVE.*

"Jesus," I whisper into the pillow, trying not to laugh.

Ethan stirs behind me, his voice a scratchy growl against my shoulder. "Are you laughing at me?"

"No," I say sweetly. "Just tallying up last night's stats."

He kisses my shoulder. "So what's the final score?"

I roll onto my back, stretch like a cat, and grin. "Five for five."

He groans. "Fuck. That's a career high. I should retire now."

"You definitely peaked," I tease.

He leans over me, hair mussed, jaw still shadowed with stubble, eyes dark with sleep and satisfaction. "I could probably get you to six."

"Oh my God," I say, laughing now. "You're insufferable."

"You *love* it."

"Okay, *maybe* a little."

He drops a kiss to my neck, then one to my collarbone, and murmurs, "Record-breaking sex and a full breakfast buffet? This might be my best day ever."

I smack his chest. "Get up, Wilson. Your victory lap is over."

We get dressed—eventually—and make our way down to the hotel restaurant, fingers brushing as we walk side by side. It feels... easy. Comfortable. Like something real. Something we've earned.

The second we round the corner into the dining area, a chorus erupts.

"OHHHHHHH!"

"Look who finally showed up!"

"There they are—Team No Sleep!"

"Did you two *break* the bed or what?"

I cover my face with both hands as Ethan grins like he's just been knighted.

Connor glares over his orange juice. "If I hear one more joke about you two... you know.. doing it... I will kill myself."

"Dude, its not us. Its them." Ethan says, sliding into the seat next to me glaring at everyone opposite us.

Maya raises an eyebrow. "You both have that orgasmic glow."

Rachel nearly chokes on her coffee. "Got to have been more than once?"

Lexi gives me a smug look. "I trained him well."

Connor visibly blanches. "Oh my God."

"I'm joking," she says, laughing. "Mostly."

I sip my coffee and try not to spontaneously combust.

Ethan throws his arm over the back of my chair like he's a smug bastard and *knows* it. "She's just jealous."

Lexi kicks him under the table. "Careful, Wilson. You wouldn't want me sharing how epic your dad is in bed now would you..."

The whole table howls.

And I swear—for the first time in what feels like forever—I just *breathe*.

The air's lighter. The weight's gone. My brother's laughing. My friends are happy. And the man I once thought I'd never be able to fully trust is beside me, coffee in one hand, his fingers tracing lazy circles against my spine with the other.

Everything feels perfect.

And for the first time since I left—

I'm exactly where I want to be.

Chapter 33

Avery

It's one of those sun-drenched, golden-filtered days where everything feels too good to be real.

The team's spread out across the stables—Connor's feeding a goat through the fence like it's a tactical exercise, Maya and Rachel are taking a thousand selfies with Titan, and Lexi's halfway in love with a horse named Maverick who keeps trying to eat her ponytail.

I'm showing them around like this is my world—which, for the first time, it actually is. Every stall I pass, every gate I open, every saddle I adjust... it feels like home.

"I still can't believe this is your job," Maya says, reaching out to stroke a mare's nose. "You're like... a horse girl in the wild."

"I prefer the term *equestrian badass*," I say, grinning.

Ethan trails behind me, quiet but smiling, watching me like I hung the moon and tacked up the stars after.

Our fingers brush a few times. Every time, my pulse spikes like a spooked filly.

I'm about to turn and show them the training ring when I hear a voice behind me.

"Quite the entourage you've got," Dan says, strolling up with a coffee in one hand and a smirk in place.

"Hey, Dan," I greet him, heart still light.

He nods toward the group. "They're clearly proud. And they should be. That was one hell of a round yesterday."

"Thanks," I say, still glowing.

Dan turns to the rest of them, projecting his voice a bit. "We're just thrilled we get to keep her for the next year. A full season with someone like Avery? It's a game-changer."

And just like that, the air shifts.

The tension is subtle—like the moment before a storm, when the sky darkens just enough to make you second-guess the sunshine.

I turn, immediately locking eyes with Ethan.

His expression—so open, so easy a second ago—drops.

Like someone unplugged the light behind his eyes.

He swallows hard, nods once, then turns and walks off toward the paddock.

My stomach plummets.

Lexi catches my glance, eyebrows furrowing slightly. Connor notices too. Everyone does. But no one says anything.

Dan, oblivious, just keeps talking. "Honestly, I thought she might head home after the first couple of months—but no, she's in. Fully committed. And we couldn't be happier."

I smile. Or at least I try.

But my insides feel like they're twisting in on themselves.

Because Ethan didn't know.

Because I didn't tell him.

Because maybe part of me didn't want to believe he'd care that much. Or worse—maybe part of me didn't want to admit that I was waiting for him to ask me to come back.

And now?

Now he thinks I made my choice.

Chapter 34

Ethan

I sit on the bench outside the stables, elbows on my knees, hands steepled together like prayer might actually help me right now.

It's not the cold steel under my palms or the faint ache in my ribs that hits hardest.

It's her voice.

Her laugh.

Echoing just a few feet away.

She's showing the team around like she's lived here forever. Confident. Glowing. Alive in a way I used to think had something to do with me.

I was wrong.

Dan's voice still rings in my ears.

"We're lucky to keep her for the next year. She's the heart of this place."

And she smiled.

Like she wanted it. Like she was staying, even despite how right we are together. Like going back with me was never even a consideration.

I close my eyes and lean forward, trying to breathe past the sharp twist in my chest.

I didn't think it would feel like this.

I thought... after everything, after showing up, after waiting, after all the fucking *trying*—I thought she might want to come home with me.

"Hey."

Connor's voice cuts through the noise. He drops onto the bench beside me without fanfare, handing me a bottle of water like I'm about to go into battle instead of just trying not to fall apart.

We don't say anything for a long time.

He just sits there.

No advice. No big brother monologue. No "I told you so."

Just him. Present. Steady. The one constant in a world that suddenly feels off its axis.

"I really thought she'd come back," I mutter eventually, my voice barely above a whisper. "That she was just waiting for the right moment to say it."

Connor leans back, kicks a pebble with his boot.

"She's figuring it out," he says finally. "Doesn't mean she doesn't care."

I nod slowly, staring out at the pasture where a couple of horses graze, totally oblivious to the mess of my heart.

"I just... don't know how to be okay without her anymore."

Connor doesn't flinch. Doesn't scoff or tease like he would've a year ago.

He just nudges my shoulder once. Solid. Quiet.

"I know."

And somehow, that's enough.

Not to fix it.

Not to make the ache go away.

But to remind me I'm not alone in it.

I stay on the bench for another few minutes, like if I sit here long enough, the weight in my chest will shift. It doesn't.

Connor doesn't push.

He just waits—calm, steady, the way he always is when he knows I'm about to make a dumb decision and need someone to stop me without making it worse.

Finally, he stands. Dusts his hands on his jeans.

"We leave in a few hours," he says, nodding toward the barn. "You gonna waste it sitting out here sulking like a kicked puppy, or you gonna come drink warm beer and eat terrible snacks with the rest of us?"

I glance up at him, brows lifting. "That's your pitch? Warm beer and disappointment?"

He shrugs. "Figured I'd stick to what I know."

A smile pulls at the corner of my mouth despite everything.

"You're a menace," I mutter, dragging a hand down my face.

"And you're a pain in the ass. Come on."

He doesn't wait for a yes. Just starts walking toward the barn like he already knows I'll follow.

And he's right.

Because as much as it feels like my chest has been hollowed out and replaced with barbed wire, I'm not about to waste the last few hours I have with the people who've kept me from completely unraveling this past month.

So I get up.

I shove the hurt down deep—where it can't quite reach my face—and I walk.

The sound of laughter hits me before I reach the door. Lexi and Rachel bickering about card games. Liam probably cheating at one. Maya judging everyone from her perch like the wine queen she is.

Avery's laugh is in there too.

It makes my ribs ache.

Inside, it's chaos in the way only this group can manage. Someone's turned up the music a little too loud. There's an open bag of marshmallows being used as poker chips. Carter is accusing everyone of cheating. Liam's somehow found a stool to stand on and is using a pool cue as a microphone.

Lexi spots me first. She smiles, small and knowing. "Hey, lover boy."

"Hi, chaos gremlin."

That earns a few groans and a snort from Carter, who's halfway through stacking the marshmallows into a pyramid.

Avery's at the far end of the makeshift table. She's laughing at something Rachel said, hand curled around a drink, hair loose around her shoulders. She hasn't looked at me yet.

I sit down anyway.

Not right beside her. Not so close it forces anything. But close enough that I can hear her exhale when I do. Close enough that it counts.

Connor tosses a half-warm can of beer my way. "You're late. Rachel already cheated twice."

"I did not cheat," Rachel says, entirely unbothered. "I just used the rules to my advantage."

"You made up the rules," Maya replies, not looking up from her cards.

"They were good rules."

"Lexi's been hoarding face cards," Carter mutters, flipping over a three with visible disgust. "Pretty sure she's running an underground blackjack ring."

"I prefer the term high-stakes strategist," Lexi says.

"Liam's the dealer and he's been singing his own theme music for fifteen minutes," Maya adds.

"I'm the vibe!" Liam yells from the stool.

The table erupts into laughter, and for a moment, it's easy. Easy to sit here and just exist with them. Like none of the rest of it is hanging over me.

I reach for a card, and so does Avery.

Our hands brush.

She pulls back first. Doesn't meet my eyes. But there's a slight lift at the corner of her mouth that wasn't there a second ago.

"I shouldn't have walked off, you have every right to chase your dreams." I say, keeping my voice low enough that only she hears.

"I'm sorry Ethan, I wanted to tell you about the contract but I just couldn't find the right moment."

"I'm not giving up on us. But I will give you your space to figure out if you have space in your life for me."

"Ethan..."

"Let's enjoy our last few hours together. I'm going to beat your ass at this game."

She finally looks at me. Just for a second. "Put your money where your mouth is then you cocky bugger."

I smile. "Let's go."

We play. Cards pass back and forth. Carter starts singing badly. Liam actually wins a round and screams about it like he's just secured Olympic gold.

Avery steals chips from Rachel. Lexi rigs the next deal. I throw a marshmallow at Connor when he accuses me of bluffing. He throws one back and hits me in the neck.

Everyone's yelling about it like it's life or death.

And Avery's laughing.

Not the polite kind. Not forced.

She's laughing like she means it. Like her guard's down for once.

And for a little while, it's like everything's okay. Like we're just a group of dysfunctional idiots wasting a Sunday afternoon in a barn full of stories and too many feelings.

And for the first time all day... I laugh.

Not because it doesn't still hurt. Not because I'm fine.

But because I'm here. With them. With her.

And maybe, just maybe, that's enough—for now.

The airport is loud—families rushing past, announcements crackling overhead, laughter and chaos everywhere.

But in this moment, everything feels still. Muted.

Because she's standing in front of me like a goodbye I don't know how to say.

Avery's arms are wrapped around her middle, like she's trying to keep all her pieces from falling apart. Like if she doesn't hold tight enough, she'll shatter. And God, I know the feeling.

The others have already said their goodbyes. Lexi kissed her cheek and whispered something only Avery could hear. Rachel, Maya, even Liam all hugged her like they were scared to let go. Connor squeezed her too tight and walked away like it didn't almost kill him.

But I can't walk away.

Not yet.

Not from her.

I step in closer, barely breathing. My heart is beating so loud it feels like the only thing in the entire terminal.

"I don't want to get on that plane," I murmur.

Avery's eyes snap to mine. Glassy. Shining. Pain-filled.

"Then don't," she whispers, even though we both know I will.

Even though we both know I have to.

I reach for her hand and thread our fingers together. "Tell me to stay and I will."

Her lips tremble. Her grip tightens. But she doesn't say it.

Because she's stronger than I am.

Because she knows that staying wouldn't fix the ache. Wouldn't make the timing right. Would only blur the lines between loving someone and losing yourself in the process.

"I want to be selfish," she says, voice barely holding. "I want to ask you to stay. I want to scream at the top of my lungs that I need you here."

"Then do it," I plead. "Say it."

She shakes her head, a tear slipping down her cheek. "But I also love you enough to let you go, I've been watching your games. You are on fire lately, I will not let you give all that up for me."

I flinch.

God, that hurts more than anything she could've said.

She lifts her chin, fighting the emotion like hell. "You came all this way to remind me that someone can still show up. That someone can still choose me. But I can't ask you to wait."

"You don't have to," I whisper. "I would give it all up for you."

Another tear falls. "You deserve more than breadcrumbs from someone who's still trying to find their footing."

I step in, resting my forehead to hers. "You're not a breadcrumb, Avery. You're my whole fucking meal."

She laughs through her tears. A soft, cracked sound. "God, you're such a mess."

"I'm your mess," I murmur. "And I'll wait. A week. A year. Ten years. I'll wait until you're ready. Just promise me you'll come back when you are, or at least let me come to you."

She doesn't promise.

She just kisses me.

It's soft and slow and full of every goodbye we don't want to say. Her hands are on my chest, mine tangled in her hair, and for a moment, it feels like maybe time really could stop. Maybe this could be our always.

But the final boarding call echoes behind me.

And she steps back.

"I have to let you go," she says quietly, tears falling freely now. "But it doesn't mean I'll ever stop loving you."

My throat burns. My chest cracks wide open.

I nod. "Just don't forget me, okay?"

She presses a kiss to my knuckles. "You're unforgettable, Ethan Wilson. That's the problem."

And when I finally turn and walk away, it feels like the hardest thing I've ever done.

Because every step toward that plane is a step away from the only person who's ever made me feel like I was worth staying for.

Chapter 35

Avery

It's been a month since they left.

Since *he* left.

One whole month since I stood in the airport parking lot, watching their plane disappear into the night—my chest cracked open and bleeding, pretending like it didn't feel like my entire world was leaving without me.

I kept it together until I made it home.

Then I fell apart.

And every day since?

I've been surviving.

Functioning.

Riding.

But I haven't *breathed.*

Not really.

The stable's quiet today. Too quiet. Titan's already worked and cooled down, my lessons are done for the morning, and the only thing left is the heavy silence of missing someone so badly your ribs ache with it.

Because I do.

God, I miss him.

His stupid smirk.

His dumb banter.

The way he always lingers like he's afraid I'll disappear if he looks away for too long.

He never stopped texting. Not once.

Not the morning after he left. Not the week after. Not even when I went silent for two days straight just to see if I could go without it.

Turns out I can't.

Every morning: *Good luck today, Aves. You're the bravest person I know.*

Every night: *Still here. Still yours. Whenever you're ready. Love you baby.*

He never asks for more. Never pushes. He just... stays.

And that's what kills me.

Because I told myself I needed space. That I couldn't give everything up for a boy—even one like him.

But what do you do when space feels worse than suffocation?

What do you do when the life you've always wanted suddenly tastes hollow because he's not here to share it?

I pick up my phone, thumb hovering over his name like I've done a hundred times this week. I don't even need to open the message thread anymore—I've memorized it. Every check-in. Every *I'm proud of you.* Every quiet *I miss you.*

A tear falls, hits the screen, and blurs his name.

I wipe it away and finally open a new message.

But I don't type *I miss you.*

I don't type *I love you*, even though it's sitting on my tongue like a goddamn secret I'm choking on.

Instead, I do the only thing I've been afraid to do since he walked out of that airport.

I call *Lexi.*

It rings twice.

"Hey," she answers, breathless. "Avery? Everything okay?"

I exhale hard. "I need your help."

She goes quiet for a second. "Okay... with what? Are you okay?"

I press a palm to my chest. My heart is hammering.

"I want to surprise him. I need to come home."

Silence. Then a slow, dangerous grin in her voice.

"Oh hell yes."

"I just... I need to... I can't do all this without him," I whisper. "Dan's agreed to release me early as long as I return for training camps. I found a similar job near home. Everything's lined up. I've made the logical choice."

"You've not been doing well without him have you." Lexi finishes gently.

"No... I miss him every day," I say. "I have everything I ever dreamed of. And I still feel empty. I don't want to just be proud of myself—I want to celebrate it *with him*. I want the stupid late-night kitchen talks. The post-practice breakdowns. The getting-to-do-life *together* part."

Lexi doesn't say *I told you so*. She doesn't need to.

"Lets get you home! Yay! I knew you two were soul mates."

I nod, tears falling again. "Yeah. I'm ready to give Ethan the grand gesture he deserves."

Because if this love is going to last—we have to *fight* for it.

And this time?

It's my turn to chase him.

Chapter 36

Avery

The plane touches down with a jolt that snaps me straight out of my anxious spiral.

I'm home.

Well, almost. The runway counts. So does the sudden urge to vomit and cry at the same time.

The seatbelt sign dings off and I grab my bag with hands that won't stop trembling..

When I push through the arrivals gate, the first thing I hear is—

"SHE'S HERE!!!"

Then chaos.

Screaming.

Actual screaming.

Lexi is the first to tackle me. Full tilt. Zero grace. Nearly knocks me into a row of baggage carts.

"You better be crying," she says, voice already thick with emotion as she squeezes me like I'm a winning lottery ticket.

"I'm absolutely crying," I whisper into her hair, laughing through tears.

Rachel's next, shoving Lexi off me just to pull me into one of her signature perfume-scented bear hugs. "My God, I forgot how hot you are in real life," she says. "What's in the water down in Louisiana? Confidence? Sex appeal? Glitter?"

"Heatstroke," I croak.

"Whatever, you look like a goddess," Maya says, giving me a quick squeeze before holding me at arm's length. "And clearly, you've been busy living your main-character equestrian dreams."

"I've missed you all so much, I know its only been a month but I need to come home."

"Duh. Of course you did." Rachel flips her sunglasses onto her head. "We're amazing."

We pile into Lexi's car like overcaffeinated high schoolers on the last day of school. The whole drive is chaos—music blaring, everyone talking over each other, throwing snacks, screaming when I mention that Ethan *still* texts me twice a day.

"You *have* to do something huge tonight," Maya says.

"Bigger than showing up at the last game of the season unannounced after flying halfway across the country?" I tease.

Lexi wiggles her brows. "We were thinking confetti cannons and maybe a flash mob."

"Or," Rachel grins, "we just casually stroll in looking hotter than sin and let Ethan spontaneously combust."

"I like that plan," I say, trying not to let my heart explode at the thought of seeing his face again. "Do the boys know anything?"

"Absolutely not," Lexi says. "Connor thinks we're at some charity thing. Mason still thinks we're picking up Rachel's grandma. The others are too busy panicking about the game to question anything."

"Perfect," I breathe. "Let's blow their damn minds."

We roll into Lexi's place and immediately break into mission mode. Dresses are flying. Hair straighteners are heating. Someone's playing a pump-up playlist that keeps alternating between sad Taylor Swift and bad bitch Beyoncé.

Somehow, it's exactly the emotional whiplash I need.

Because tonight?

It's game time.

For *me*.

Lexi's Apartment – 6:32pm

"Okay, we've got an hour until puck drop," Lexi announces like she's a drill sergeant in a fashion bootcamp. "Everyone has twenty minutes to become dangerously hot. Let's move!"

I'm already halfway through curling the last piece of my hair, sitting on her bed in front of her massive mirror that doubles as a motivational speech every time I look at it. Because tonight?

Tonight I look good.

Like *drop-dead, soul-snatching, no-you-can't-have-my-number* good.

Black skinny jeans that hug in all the right places. Little black boots with just enough heel to say *I'm hot but I'll still kick your ass.* And on top? Ethan's jersey.

Number 21.

It drowns me, hangs off one shoulder, and still somehow manages to be the sexiest thing I've ever worn.

"You're a menace," Lexi says when she walks in and sees me.

Rachel appears behind her, blinking like she just walked into a Victoria's Secret ad. "Oh no, he's gonna die."

Maya whistles. "Funeral's at nine. Wear black."

I laugh, but my chest is tight. My heart's rattling in my ribcage like it's got a grudge. I run a hand over Ethan's name on the back of the jersey and take a slow, deep breath.

"You good?" Lexi asks, stepping into the room and fixing a wavy strand that's fallen into my face.

"I think so," I say. "I just... want tonight to matter. I want him to see how much I need him."

Lexi wraps her arms around me from behind, chin on my shoulder. "He already know's. Tonight's just the *mic drop.*"

Rachel walks past, clutching a bottle of champagne. "And I brought props for the after party."

"Focus!" Lexi calls after her. "Eyes on the prize. Sexy vengeance and romantic redemption first, drunk karaoke later."

The apartment smells like curling irons, hairspray, and high-stakes adrenaline. Maya's fixing her lip gloss in the hallway mirror, Rachel's dancing to Beyoncé in the kitchen, and Lexi's adjusting her earrings like she's going into battle.

And me?

I'm about to walk into the last game of the season in the jersey of the man I love.

Chapter 37

Ethan

Pre-game Warm Ups – Last Game of the Season

The sound of my blades carving across the ice should be the best kind of therapy. Normally, it is. That rhythmic glide, the bite of cold in my lungs, the roar of the crowd starting to build like thunder in the background.

But not tonight.

Tonight, it feels like I'm skating through fog.

Physically? I'm fine. Mentally? Focused. But emotionally? I'm fucking wrecked.

Because this is it. Last game of the season. We win, we finish top of the league. A season to remember. Redemption. Glory.

And yet... I'd give it all up just to see her in the stands.

Connor claps a hand on my shoulder as we pass each other, eyes sharp like always. But there's softness there too—one only I get to see.

"You good?" he mutters.

I nod. Too fast. Too fake. "Yeah."

Liam slides in beside us. "You're skating like you've got lead in your pants, bro."

"Shut up."

"You need a pre-game hug?" he teases.

I elbow him. Hard. "I need you to stop breathing near me."

He laughs but shoots me a look that lingers too long. Yeah. They see it. All of them do.

The ache. The empty.

The Avery-shaped hole in my goddamn chest.

It's not that she's gone-gone. She texts me. Every day. Morning and night like clockwork. And I live for those messages. But it's not the same. It's not her curled into my side. It's not her lip curled in sass, or her laugh across the locker room.

It's not waking up to her bare skin tangled in my sheets.

It's not *us*.

I skate a few more drills, trying to pull myself back into it. The team's dialled in. Focused. Locked. This game is everything. And I owe it to them to show the hell up.

Right as I lean over to grab a water bottle off the boards, my phone buzzes in my coat pocket.

Coach is still in the office. I check it. Quick glance.

Avery 🩰

Good luck out there, Wilson. I wish I could be there to watch you dominate one more time. You've got this. Proud of you, always.

Goddamn.

I stare at the message a little too long.

Liam catches me.

"Still breaking your heart, huh?"

I shove my phone away. "Just don't fuck up the first period."

But even as I skate back out onto the ice, the words stick to me like armor.

Proud of you, always.

I'm going to play this game like it's not just the championship on the line.

I'm going to play for her.

Let's fucking go.

Chapter 38

Ethan

This isn't how it was supposed to go.

We're down 2–1 and playing like we forgot how to hold our sticks. My legs feel like concrete, my passes are half a second too late, and I'm skating like I've got fog in my brain.

Every time I glance at the stands, I swear I see her.

But it's never her.

Just shadows and ghosts and memories of Avery.

The girl I let walk away.

She texted me before warmups—*"Wish I could be there to watch you dominate."*

Like it was casual. Like it didn't gut me.

Because this game?

This win?

None of it means shit without her.

The buzzer sounds, dragging us into the first intermission, and no one's talking. Carter's jaw is locked. Mason slams his stick against the boards on his way to the bench.

And me? I feel like my chest's about to cave in.

We're halfway to the tunnel when my dad—Coach to the rest of the world—holds up a hand. "Hold up."

The whole team slows to a stop like we just hit a wall.

"You're not heading in yet," he calls, loud enough for the arena to hear.

Carter frowns. "What now?"

Dad's smiling. Just slightly. And that's worse. **That's dangerous.**

"Before you go," he continues, "we've got a guest in the building. A very special guest. And I think this moment calls for a photo."

The crowd ripples with murmurs. The Jumbotron shifts to a wide shot of the ice. Everyone's watching.

Liam leans in, low voice. "Please be a dog. Or pizza. Or a dog delivering pizza."

No such luck.

Dad gestures toward the tunnel. "Let's give a warm welcome..."

And the lights dim.

The arena hushes.

A spotlight hits the edge of the tunnel.

My heart stops.

And then—

Boots.

Black. Laced. Perfectly worn. Stepping out like a goddamn dream.

The crowd gasps as the spotlight pans up her legs—tight black jeans, **my jersey**, hair down and glowing like it's been kissed by the sun itself.

And then her face.

Avery.

The arena **erupts**.

It's like time fractures. Sound and movement blur around her as she steps out slowly, looking every bit like the girl who's haunted my nights for the last month. My girl.

Her eyes scan the ice—and then they find me.

And it's like the whole fucking world stops spinning.

I don't move.

Can't move.

The team's staring. The crowd's screaming. The announcer's saying something but it's just static in my ears.

Because all I see is her.

And in her eyes?

That flicker. That fire. That *possibility* I thought I lost.

Liam elbows me. "Dude. Say something. Blink. Breathe. Anything."

But I'm already skating forward—slow, like if I move too fast, she'll disappear.

She smiles. Small. Nervous. Wrecked. Radiant.

And I swear to God, I've never seen anything so beautiful.

She smiles.

And that's it.

I drop my stick without thinking.

Helmet off. Gloves forgotten.

Like nothing else matters.

Because it doesn't.

Not this game.

Not the thousand people watching from the stands or the millions who'll see the photos tomorrow.

Just her.

She meets me halfway, boots thudding on the ice, her steps unsure but her eyes never wavering. And when she's close enough for me to touch—

I stop.

One breath.

Two.

Her lips tremble, but she doesn't look away. "Surprise."

I laugh, and it comes out cracked and broken and half a sob. "Jesus, Avery."

She shrugs. "You said you'd wait for me."

"I would've waited forever."

"I didn't want you to."

She's crying now, tears spilling down her pink cheeks.

"I couldn't breathe without you," she whispers. "Couldn't sleep. Couldn't think. And then Lexi said—she said I looked like someone who forgot what home felt like."

"And?"

Her voice shatters. "And you're my home, Ethan."

The roar from the crowd fades to white noise. My chest caves in with the force of it.

I step closer. Hands on her face. Forehead to hers. My thumbs brush tears off her cheeks as she clutches my jersey like she might fall without it.

"I didn't know how to fix it," I say. "I didn't know how to make you stay."

"You didn't have to," she says. "You just had to show up and be there for me."

My lips crash into hers.

And the arena disappears.

She melts into me, arms wrapped tight around my neck, the kiss so deep and desperate it tastes like a second chance. Like forgiveness. Like every 'almost' we ever had finally coming true.

The crowd goes absolutely ballistic.

Somewhere, I hear the guys whooping, someone shouting, "That's our boy!"

But I don't care.

I'm kissing her like she's oxygen and I've been drowning since the day she left.

And she's kissing me like she never wants to come up for air again.

When we finally break apart, we're breathless. Shaking. Wrecked.

"I love you," I murmur, voice raw. "I don't need time or space or signs from the universe. I just need you."

She smiles, still tear-streaked and glowing.

"You have me," she says. "But you better go win this game. Or I'm leaving again."

I laugh through the burn in my throat. "You really are a devil."

She kisses me one more time. Soft. Slow. Soul-stealing.

"Now go," she whispers, smoothing a hand down my jersey. "Show them who you are."

And with the whole damn world watching—

I skate back to the team. Just to hear her shout "And Ethan..." I look back at her "I love you too!"

And a fire in my chest like nothing I've ever known.

I hit the ice like I've been reborn.

The second period starts and I can already hear her—Avery—somewhere in the crowd. I don't need to see her to feel her. She's a fucking gravity well, and I'm locked in orbit.

The puck drops, and something clicks.

I'm not skating anymore—I'm flying. Cutting through defenders like they're cardboard cutouts. Every pass finds me. Every shot hits tape. I take one on the rush, deke left, cut right, and snipe it top shelf like I've been waiting all season for this exact second.

3–2.

The arena erupts.

I don't celebrate. I glance up instead—eyes scanning until I catch her.

She's on her feet, screaming like her whole damn soul's on fire. And when our eyes lock?

I smile.

And then I destroy.

By the end of the third period, I've got a hat trick and an assist. By mid-third, Liam buries a beauty and yells, "That one's for Avery!" like the dramatic little shit he is.

The other team's falling apart. We're skating circles around them. Connor even lets a chirp slip: "You boys wanna borrow our bench? Might be safer there."

We rack up goal after goal.

6–2.

7–2.

The crowd's deafening.

8–2.

And that last one? Yeah, I pass it off. Because winning's good—but watching Liam score the final goal, fist-pumping the air while he points straight at Avery in the stands?

That's unforgettable.

The buzzer sounds, and the arena explodes.

We've done it.

Top of the league.

Undeniable. Unstoppable. Un-fucking-believable.

I rip my helmet off and toss my stick. The team swarms. Shouts and sweaty hugs and Liam screaming, "WE DID IT, BABY!" while Mason tries to tackle the entire bench.

But me?

I turn to the glass.

She's there. Still glowing. Still mine.

And for the first time in a long damn time—

I feel like I've finally won everything I ever wanted.

Flashes go off like fireworks the second I step into the media room. Microphones everywhere. Cameras clicking. Reporters shouting over each other like it's a damn auction.

I just scored a hat trick, broke a league record, and helped my team clinch the top spot. But none of that's why I'm sweating.

Because she's out there. Somewhere.

Watching.

I wipe my mouth, sit down, and lean into the mic.

First question hits: "Ethan, hell of a night. That second period looked like you flipped a switch. What changed?"

I pause.

Think of her.

Then smile. Small. Private. The kind that starts in your chest and leaks into your eyes.

"You ever feel like you're living in the penalty box?" I say, voice low but steady. "Like no matter how hard you skate, no matter how many goals you score, you're still sitting out when it matters most?"

The room quiets.

"That was me. For years. I lived fast, played harder, but I never really *felt* the game. Not the way I did tonight."

I glance down, swallow.

"Sometimes, one person walks into your life and makes it make sense. And when they leave... you feel it everywhere. In your chest. Your legs. Your hands. But if you're lucky enough to get another shot—you take it."

A pause. A breath. My eyes lift to the camera like I'm speaking to *her*.

"When you find the person who lights up your soul, the one who makes every penalty worth it, every scar make sense? You don't let them go. You fight like hell. And you win for them."

Dead silence.

Someone whispers, "Holy shit," off-mic.

Another reporter clears their throat, voice gentler now. "Was this the beautiful young woman we saw you with on the ice today?"

I just smile. "Yes, and I want everyone to know how lucky I am to have everything I could ever want. I got the win and I got the girl."

Then I stand, thank them, and walk off the stage like I didn't just confess my entire heart to a stadium full of reporters.

I leave the podium still vibrating from that last question. My legs are moving, but I'm not sure where I'm going. I just know I need air. Space.

Her.

The hallway outside the media room is quiet—just the low hum of electricity and the distant echo of fans pouring out of the arena.

And then I see her.

She's standing under one of the low, flickering lights in the tunnel that leads to the player's exit. Hands tucked into the sleeves of my jersey—the same one I watched her wear from across the ice, lighting me up like a goddamn beacon.

Her hair's a little messy. Eyes glassy. And when she sees me—*really* sees me—her whole face folds in on itself, like she's been holding back a flood and one look at me cracked the dam.

I walk.

Then jog.

Then I'm running.

No hesitation. No plan.

Just *her*.

I don't stop until my hands are on her cheeks and her arms are around my waist and we're crashing into each other like the world might stop spinning if we don't.

"I saw the press conference," she whispers, breathless against my chest.

I nod, forehead to hers, voice rough. "Meant every word."

She laughs—choked, teary, beautiful. "You didn't have to say all that on national TV."

"I did. Because for the first time in my life, I wanted *everyone* to know I love someone more than I love the game."

She blinks up at me, stunned.

My thumb wipes under her eye where a tear's slipped free. "You lit up my whole fucking soul, Avery Maddox. And I'll spend every damn day proving I deserve you."

And then she kisses me.

Right there in the tunnel. Where the echoes of skates and fans and victory still hum in the air. Where I first walked out broken, and now I stand whole.

Because she came back.

Because this time—we're doing it right.

Chapter 39

Ethan

The sun's barely up.

Golden light spills across the hardwood floor of my new apartment—*our* apartment—and paints her bare shoulder like a damn masterpiece. She's curled up in my t-shirt, legs tangled in the sheets, her hair a riot of waves on my pillow.

I don't move.

Don't even breathe too loud.

Because waking up next to Avery Maddox feels like winning a championship I didn't know I was playing for. Like every moment I spent hurting, missing her, losing sleep over whether we'd ever get here—*this*—was worth it.

She shifts, then groans softly and blinks at me.

"Creep," she mumbles, voice full of sleep and sass. "How long have you been staring at me?"

"At least ten minutes. I'd say sorry but I'm not."

She stretches—arms up, shirt riding high, the most perfect goddamn sight I've ever seen. "We're really doing this, huh?"

I grin and drag my fingers gently down her thigh. "We've been doing it for three months now, baby. But yeah. Now we've got fresh sheets, no Connor under the same roof, and a brand-new coffee maker I don't know how to work. This is the real deal."

She snorts. "I can't believe you made me move in after, like, one night."

"One *life-altering, soul-healing, tree-climbing sex marathon* night," I correct.

Her laugh is muffled by my chest as she flops on top of me. "God, you're annoying in the morning."

"You love me."

"Tragically."

We lie there like that for a while—her sprawled across me, my arms wrapped around her like she might float away if I let go.

Her hand slides over my heart and stays there, like she's trying to memorize the way it beats for her.

"I'm never going anywhere without you ever again," she whispers.

I smile. "Good. Because I already threw out the return policy."

The car is chaos.

Lexi's yelling at Ethan from the front seat about playing a prank on one of the rookies. Maya's got her feet on my lap in the back, giggling like she's already three mimosas deep (she's not), and Rachel's wedged between us, scrolling TikTok with the volume up like we're not all in a moving vehicle together.

Ethan catches my eye in the rearview mirror and smirks. I blow him a kiss, and he winks like the cocky menace he is.

The team's celebrating the end of the season—and more importantly, that win. The one that put them at the top of the league. And Connor, naturally, insisted on hosting at his place. Said it was tradition.

More like *control freak syndrome,* but hey, he makes a mean garlic bread.

When we finally pull up to the building, everyone piles out like clowns from a circus car. Carter and Liam are already waiting outside, and from the sound of the music upstairs, the party's well underway.

We take the elevator, Ethan's hand warm and familiar in mine. I can't stop smiling.

This is it.

This feeling.

My favorite people. My city. My life coming together in a way that doesn't make me ache anymore.

The second we step into Connor's apartment, I'm hit with the smell of something amazing—probably food dad made because let's be honest, Lexi is no good in the kitchen.

The place is packed. Jerseys, jeans, champagne bottles—it's a blur of happy chaos. Laughter bounces off the walls, someone's already dared Mason to shotgun a beer, and someone else (probably Carter) is yelling about who cheated in beer pong last time.

But then I spot him.

Connor.

Standing in the kitchen with a towel over his shoulder and an apron that says *Grill Sergeant.* And next to him?

Rachel.

Laughing at something he just said, cheeks pink, eyes shining like she actually enjoys his presence.

Oh no.

Oh no no no.

Connor's looking at her like she's the eighth wonder of the world. Like she just solved world peace *and* offered him a cold beer.

I elbow Lexi and nod toward them. "Is my brother still in love with Rachel?"

She sips her wine. "Connor's been in love with Rachel since she told him to shut up with a glitter pen in sophomore year and will probably still be in love with her when he 6 feet under."

Maya snorts. "He's just slow to commit to the bit."

Rachel turns and catches me watching—gives me a wink and a shrug that says *yep, your brother's obsessed with me, what of it?*

I shrug back. *You're welcome, honestly.*

Ethan wraps his arms around my waist from behind, resting his chin on my shoulder. "You good?"

I lean back into him. "Perfect."

And I mean it.

Every second of it.

This is everything I have ever wanted.

Chapter 40

Ethan

12 Months Later

There are moments in life that feel like dreams.

And then there are moments like this—too vivid, too perfect to be anything but real.

Our apartment hums with quiet. Warm, soft light filters through the balcony doors, spilling across the hardwood like it's wrapping the room in gold. My gear bag drops to the floor with a dull thud, but she doesn't turn around.

She's out there—barefoot, leaning against the railing like a postcard from a better life.

Her hair's down, wild from the breeze, curling around her shoulders. She's wearing one of my hoodies. The same one she stole during playoffs and claimed as her own.

My lungs ache just looking at her.

Because she's it. My before. My after. My forever.

I step out onto the balcony, quiet, reverent, like I'm approaching something sacred.

"Hey," I say softly, wrapping my arms around her from behind.

She leans into me without hesitation. No hesitation, ever. Just her whole body melting into mine like it belongs here.

"Tough day?" she murmurs.

"Only until I saw you," I breathe against her skin.

Her hands cover mine, fingers threading through. She exhales, and there's something about the way she does it—like she's holding in a secret.

I turn her gently in my arms.

And the second I see her eyes, I know.

She's glowing. Not just in the sunset—but in that way you feel in your bones.

"I love you," she says first. Just that. Simple. Soft. Sure.

"I love you too," I whisper, brushing my thumb across her cheek. "So damn much."

She bites her lip and takes my hand. Presses it flat over her stomach.

"I'm pregnant, Ethan."

I blink.

The world stills.

"I—what?"

"I took three tests," she laughs through the tears starting to well in her eyes. "All positive."

She's crying.

I think I am too.

My heart stutters, skips, then takes off like it's breaking through my chest.

"We're having a baby?" I say, just to hear it out loud. Just to believe it.

She nods, and I swear the air leaves my lungs.

I lift her off the ground, burying my face in her neck, holding her like the whole world depends on it.

Because it does.

"I didn't think I could love you more," I whisper into her hair. "But somehow... somehow I do."

She wraps her arms around my shoulders, tighter than ever before. "I was scared to tell you. I didn't want to change anything—we're so happy."

"You didn't change anything," I say, pulling back to look at her. "You just made the best thing in my life even better."

She laughs through another tear, and I kiss it off her cheek.

"When did this become our life?" I ask, breathless.

"When we stopped running from it," she whispers.

I press my forehead to hers, hands still resting over the new life growing between us. The future we never expected but now can't imagine not having.

"Whatever happens," I say, "however chaotic or messy or terrifying this gets—I'll be right here."

She smiles through the tears.

"I know," she says. "That's the only reason I'm not completely freaking out right now."

I grin, but I'm already crying again.

"I'm gonna build you both a home," I promise. "One you never have to leave. One that's safe. One where you'll always know how loved you are."

Her eyes shine.

"You already did," she says softly. "Right here."

And just like that... I know we'll be okay.

More than okay.

We're building a legacy out of love, out of healing, out of something that survived every storm.

There's a heartbeat inside her that's half me, half her—and all hope.

And somehow... that tiny heartbeat already feels like the loudest, strongest thing in the world.

Bonus Scene

Connor's POV

Six Months Later

You know what no one tells you?

That your best friend and your little sister falling in love is like being permanently stuck between wanting to high five someone and throw them off a bridge.

Don't get me wrong—I'm happy for them. Genuinely. Ethan's my brother in all but blood, and Avery... she's my kid sister, but she's also this fierce, unstoppable force of nature who's spent half her life proving she doesn't need anyone.

So yeah, watching the two of them build this life together—one that doesn't involve running or hiding or emotional landmines—it's kind of magic.

But still. It's weird as hell.

I knock on their apartment door with a six-pack under one arm and a pizza box balanced in the other, because I'm a damn good guest and also because I know Avery's pregnancy cravings have officially turned her into a hormonal carb goblin.

The door swings open and Ethan's standing there, grinning like a man who got laid before breakfast and knows he's got leftovers waiting in the fridge.

"Hey," he says, stepping aside. "She's out on the balcony. Sunset's her new obsession."

I nod, dropping the pizza on the counter and cracking a beer before heading outside.

There she is.

Curled up on one of those cushy outdoor chairs, legs tucked under her, bump just visible beneath her hoodie. Her hair's down, wild and a little wind-tangled, and she's got that faraway look she used to get before a big riding comp.

Except this time, she's not preparing to break records.

She's growing a whole-ass human.

I sit beside her, tipping my beer back and following her gaze to the horizon. The sky's pink and gold and too damn perfect.

"You good?" I ask.

She nods, then smirks. "You mean aside from the fact I cry at car commercials and can't eat chicken without vomiting?"

I snort. "Being pregnant is terrifying."

"You're telling me."

We're quiet for a beat. The kind of quiet only siblings can share without it being weird. Then she glances over.

"You were right, you know."

"About what?"

"Everything. About him. About me needing to go figure my shit out first. About letting myself want something real."

I don't say anything, just give her a nod, because if I open my mouth, I'll probably get sentimental and we can't have that.

"And you," she adds. "Don't think I haven't noticed how you've been around more. Helping out. Talking to Dad again. You're getting your shit together too, big bro."

"I had a good example," I mutter.

She smiles. "We're okay, right? You and me?"

I raise an eyebrow. "Even after you made me punch my best friend in the face and then made me watch him basically become a golden retriever in love?"

She laughs. "So... that's a yes?"

I lean back and clink my beer bottle against her water. "Yeah, Ave. We're more than okay."

A second later, Ethan slides the door open and steps outside, all easy charm and quiet warmth. He drops a kiss on her head like it's the most natural thing in the world, then tosses me a knowing look.

I roll my eyes. "Gross."

"You love it," he says.

"I tolerate it. Barely."

Avery reaches for his hand and laces their fingers together like they've done it a thousand times.

And maybe that's when it really hits me.

They're not just in love.

They have both finally found their place in this world.

The three of us sit there as the sun dips below the skyline, the air soft and filled with whatever this feeling is—peace maybe, or the calm before everything changes again.

And for the first time in a long time, I let myself think...

Maybe my time's coming too.

Who knows.

Maybe the next time I open my door, the girl who'll wreck me in the best possible way is standing on the other side.

God help her.

Thank You for Reading

If you made it here—thank you. Truly.

This story was about healing, about choosing yourself, and about learning that love doesn't always show up perfectly... but it can show up patiently. I hope something in these pages made you feel seen. I hope it reminded you that it's okay to be messy and brave and still deserving of a soft landing.

If this book stayed with you, even just a little, I'd love to hear from you. Your words, your reviews, and your support mean more than you know. They help stories like this find the readers who need them most.

Thank you for spending time with these characters. For holding their flaws. For rooting for their redemption.

And most of all—thank you for being here.

Printed in Great Britain
by Amazon